Canopy Row

Canopy Row

Brian Jonathan Sky

First Edition
Published by Salt Shaker Books a division of Salt Shaker Media
United States ÷ United Kingdom ÷ Canada
First published in the United States of America by Salt Shaker Books 2018

Cataloged at The Library of Congress as follows:

Canopy Row/by Brian Jonathan Sky.

ISBN-10: 0692959041
ISBN-13: 9780692959046

1. Novel/Memoir 2. Young Adult. 3. Drama 4. Homeless Teens 5. Spirituality
6. Inspirational

Printed and bound in the United States of America.
Library of Congress Control Number: 2018900342
Salt Shaker, Fort Collins, CO

Certain names and identifying characteristics have been changed whether it is so noted in the text or not, and certain characters, and events have been compressed or reordered.

For Pamela Annie, my love and partner in adventure who said, "write it."

She gave me the space, time, and encouragement, so I did.

"I should like to speak of God not on the boundaries but at the center, not in weakness but in strength, and therefore not in death and guilt but in man's life and goodness. God is the beyond in the midst of our life, and the church stands, not at the boundaries where human powers give out, but in the midst of the village."

Dietrich Bonhoeffer

Prologue

When I was nine years old I was sure I was going to make the wonder of birds my lifelong academic pursuit and be the next John James Audubon. I was fortunate that all manner of birds who were migrating from the southern hemisphere flew along the Central Flyway, and that the Central Flyway generally followed the Great Plains in the United States and Canada with El Paso, Texas being right in its path. We were treated to birds that most people only saw in books or National Geographic documentaries. That was it. I longed to be an ornithologist and a naturalist, nothing more.

I was a child of the early morning and the dusk -- prime bird watching hours. I was a child of the trees and of the fields, wandering freely along dirt roads and irrigation canals, weaving in and out of the cotton fields of West Texas as I followed and observed the birds.

This is where the story should begin -- in a place called St. Margaret's Home for Children. It was my first home. We were a blended family of nationalities and races. We were global before global became a buzzword, and we were safe, loved, and inspired. That was before the deluge, and it is after that where the story begins.

PART ONE

CHAPTER 1

Tall lanky palm trees were bending before the wind as it went whipping through the neighborhood. From inside a young boy looked out of the living room window at the rows of houses that made up his block and sighed. Life had been great -- perfect even. Then the deluge came, and swept him into the rapids that threw him gasping for air on a foreign shore. He might as well have moved to Uranus. There was a huge difference between the desert of West Texas and the coastline of Southern California. Nothing was familiar, and it had all happened so fast.

Ben put on the only school clothes he had -- the uniform he had worn at Our Lady of the Valley Parochial School. He stood looking at himself in the mirror. An internal nudge told him to lose the sweater and the tie, yet he still felt way over dressed. He grabbed his book bag and started off on what felt like a death march to school.

There were only a few cars in the school parking lot when he arrived. Ben had intentionally gotten to the school early so he could survey the layout of the place. He stationed himself along a wall and waited for the students to arrive. When the students began to show up, his concern about being over dressed was confirmed. Ben felt an impulse surge through him to run, to escape, now!

Yet he stayed as the tsunami of tanned teens engulfed him on their way to class, leaving him standing alone in the corridor. He looked at his schedule and tried to figure out the way to his homeroom.

"Can I help you?" Ben looked up to see a girl smiling. Her hair was still wet like she had just stepped out of the shower. She smelled like coconuts and had the whitest teeth he had ever seen. He temporarily developed lockjaw. Finally, he motioned to his schedule. The girl took it and looked it over. "Come on, I'm going by your room." "Oh, sucks to be you. You're in Murphy's homeroom."

The girl pointed to his classroom and walked on to get to her class. Ben watched her walk away and then slipped into the room and found a desk. His white shirt was acting like a blazing spotlight blaring; "new kid!"

Ms. Valdez, the young student teacher, began to take roll. When she came to Ben, he stood up to acknowledge his presence just as he had for as long as he had been going to school. The room got quiet as everyone turned to look at him.

"Do you need something? Asked the student teacher.

"Uh, no, you called my name so I stood up," replied Ben.

It was an awkward moment for everyone. Ben stood waiting for Ms. Valdez to tell him to be seated, and the student teacher was confused as to how to respond. She wasn't sure if Ben was being respectful or making fun of her. She opted to be positive, and responded to the respect. "Thank you, Ben, please sit down," and continued calling roll.

The class started snickering and chatter quickly followed. When the next student was called, he stood up like Ben had done. The classroom burst out with hoots and wisecracks that spiraled into total chaos. Ms. Valdez tried valiantly to restore order. Whatever order there had been, had totally deteriorated. All of a sudden a voice boomed from the back of the classroom.

"Enough!" The class instantly froze. It was like an Arctic wind had blasted in and turned the room into a polar vortex. Nobody moved. Not even the student who had stood up to mimic Ben -- and it was to him, that Mrs. Murphy directed her attention. He was now her prey.

She slowly circled the room trying to pick up a scent that might give her a clue to what had led to the commotion. Finally, she stopped directly in front of the student and calmly asked, "why are you standing, Donald?"

Don started stammering and stuttering an answer that was completely incoherent. He looked around for support from his classmates, which was useless because everyone was sitting at their desks with their eyes diverted. Nobody wanted to draw the angry teacher's attention. Ben sat taking everything in and was too amazed at what was happening to feel any sense of fear. That was at least until Mrs. Murphy bellowed, "speak up, boy!"

The entire class jumped and a deep silence fell upon the room. Don was not giving the class up. He decided to be the fall guy and deal with the consequences. Mrs. Murphy grabbed him by the shirt collar and dragged him out of the room and toward the principal's office. Her admonishments echoed off the corridor walls long after she had left the room.

When she returned, Mrs. Murphy conferenced with the student teacher outside of the classroom. The students could see Ms. Valdez gesturing with her hands and describing what had gone on. The teacher stood with her hands on her wide hips and glared into the room. She scanned the room until her gaze fell on Ben and then headed back into the classroom and straight to his desk. "Mr. Storm is it?" "Mr. Ben Storm?"

Ben stood up as he had before, sending the class into panic mode. They were fully expecting Mrs. Murphy to go ballistic on him. Instead, she placed her hand on Ben's shoulder and with a kind tone to her voice said, "We're glad to have you in our class, welcome to Alvarado. " She quickly reverted to her former self and began barking out directions and administered the punishment for the class' behavior.

When the sentencing had passed, Ben sat at his desk and wished she had not done that. He was sure that he would be labeled with non-flattering names and sent to the outer regions of kooksville.

Then a miracle happened. During lunch break, Don came over to him.

"Ok, now that was hilarious! What was with the standing up thing? You really had Ms. Valdez going."

"It's what I've been doing since I was in first grade, Ben replied. "Everybody at my school did that. We stand up when teachers call on us."

"Seriously?" exclaimed Don. "Where did you come from?"

"Texas," Ben answered. "I've just moved in with my uncle and aunt."

As Ben and Don were talking, three boys in his class came over to get Don so they could start the football game. "Let's go, game's on!" shouted Kenny.

Don motioned for Ben to follow and led him over to the field. "You can play halfback," he said.

That day on the field, his speed and ability resulted in him catching two passes for touchdowns. He then followed Don's blocking and scampered into the end zone for another. Word got around the school that the new kid was a bit different but man, could he run.

At bedtime Ben lay on the living room couch emotionally exhausted. He wondered what had happened to the big house that he'd been told about; the one where he would have his own room. He thought about his friends at the Home back in Texas. At least there he had his own space even if he did share the dorm with three other boys.

"How did this happen?" Ben felt betrayed by the nuns and especially by Mrs. Grace. After all, she was a social worker. She should have known better. With that thought floating through his waning consciousness, he drifted off to sleep and dreamt crazy, unsettling dreams about loss and uncertainty.

CHAPTER 2

The first week of school was over. Ben had survived -- barely. He had a few moments where he experienced some hope that he just might be able to fit in. Mostly, it was touch and go. He was doing a mental play-by-play review of the week in his head as he walked to Don's house, when there she was again -- the girl who had rescued him on the first day of school. She was walking on the opposite side of the street.

"Hey!" he called out.

The girl stopped. Ben walked over to her.

"It's me, the guy you helped get to class, remember?" Ben said.

"Yeah, I do. How's it going Tex?" "Boy, you made a note worthy entrance in Murphy's class. Talk is you baited the dragon and survived. Very impressive."

"Tex?" "My name's Ben." "I didn't bait the dragon, ah Mrs. Murphy."

The girl punched him in the arm. "Regardless, you're front page news, oh, and my name is Katy. Where are you going?"

Ben looked at his watch and then reached in his back pocket. "I'm heading to Dennis', some of us guys are getting together. I'm close to this street, right."

He realized that this was how they first met. "I'm not always lost, really."

Katy took the paper. "2413 Galatina, you went two streets too far. Make a "U" and turn right. Dennis' house is at the end of the street. Watch out for those guys. They can get way crazy."

"Maybe you should show me how to get there. What if I get lost again?"

It was a pathetic attempt to get Katy to stay around longer -- but it worked. She walked with him until they got to Dennis' street and left. He was left standing there sniffing the paper which now was coconut scented as a result of her having touched it.

"See you Monday, Tex." Katy called as she crossed the street.

Ben quickly dropped the paper. Had she seen him? When she turned and walked away, he bent over, picked up the paper, gave it one more whiff and placed it back in his pocket.

Don was waiting for him in the front yard when Ben walked up. "Ben's here!" He shouted to the guys. "Get the bag."

Ken and Dennis came out of the house. Ken was carrying a department store bag and walked over to him. "Here, this is from me and Dennis, Don would have chipped in, but well, look at him, he's a giant!"

Ben took the bag and looked inside and then looked up at the guys. "Clothes?" You bought me clothes?" "Why?" Asked Ben.

Ken reached in the bag and pulled out one of the shirts. "Remember when you told us about having to wear uniforms from your old school, and how your uncle wouldn't get you any new clothes?"

Ben nodded and started digging in the bag to see what else was in it. He pulled out two pairs of Levi jeans and two pairs of Levi cords. There were also six or so surfer t-shirts and two Hang Ten shirts. The guys had also included a couple of pairs of tennis shoes and a baseball cap.

Ken handed Ben back the shirt he had pulled out of the bag.

"It's just some stuff Dennis and I had hanging around. You're about our size so we figured they might fit you."

Ben was speechless. Most people may have taken this gesture of kindness as an insult and rejected the used clothes. Ben though, was so sick of wearing his lame green uniform pants and white shirt to school that the clothes he had just been given may as well have come from Macy's.

"I've hated leaving my uncle's house every morning to go to school because of how I looked. Some of the kids at school were giving me weird looks."

The guys looked at each other with relief. They hadn't been sure how Ben would react and were even afraid of offending him.

They broke out in smiles. "Try them on!"

Ben stripped down to his BVD's right there in the front yard, and chose a pair of cords, a Hang Ten shirt and the Vans. He placed a hand in a pocket of the cords and struck a pose.

"What do you think?" he asked.

Don walked over and circled around Ben. "Not too shabby."

Later, at A's Burgers, Ken gave Ben one more bit of advice. "Ben, you don't have to stand up when teachers call on you and you don't have to call them Ma'am or Sir."

The orientation continued as the guys clued Ben in on how not to stand out or be a dweeb in middle school.

Then he added. "By the way, there's a party at Susie's next week. You're going with us."

CHAPTER 3

K en and the guys hung out with a group composed of jocks along with some beautiful girls. They were accepting, but they all seemed to have the understanding that they were better that the rest of the students. No one bothered to challenge that understanding, at least among the students. The ones that were in the group were glad to be so while those that weren't, dreamt of the day when they would be ushered in like someone waiting to win some humongous social sweepstakes.

The guys were only three of the ten or so boys in the group, but they were the best looking and the most popular, and now because they had befriended Ben, he was in.

Ben was thinking about this as he walked to school one day. He was marveling at the good fortune that had befallen him. Ben wasn't aware of it, but he was walking like he'd seen Ken walk. One hand was in the pocket of his Levis and he was taking slow steps and walking in a laid back manner. He was trucking ---- he no longer walked like a tin soldier and he no longer wore his school uniform. He'd gone from being a hick to being slick in a matter of a week. It was like an elite search and rescue team had been deployed to pull him out of isolation into total inclusion.

"Jesus, Mary, and Joseph!" he thought.

A commotion was going on when Ben arrived on campus. He walked over to where a large crowd had gathered and saw that it was two girls going at it. Ben recognized one of them -- the one getting her butt kicked. The other girl was at least twice her size and had her classmate tightly by her hair and swinging her around at will. Ben was about to step in when an arm reached out and stopped him. He turned around and saw that it was Don.

"Hold on, Tex. You don't want any of this." He pulled Ben toward the edge of the crowd and tried to lead him away from the fight.

"We have to do something. That girl is getting pounded by that Amazon," yelled Ben.

Don calmly kept walking with Ben in tow. "It's just another cat fight. It's none of our business. Some teacher will be there soon. Let's get to class."

Later, Ben sat at his desk thinking about what he had just seen. A giant girl was knocking the heck out of her undersized opponent and the crowd loved it. This would have never happened at Our Lady of the Valley School. He hurt for the small girl who despite her gutsy performance was taking a beating. The fact that he could no longer hear jeering and cheering going on told him that a teacher had arrived. Regardless, he knew he should have stepped in and stopped the fight. He knew better and now felt ashamed. At one point during the fight he thought he had seen the girl give him a desperate look. He wrote a note to Don and dropped it next to his desk.

"Who was that horse beating up on that girl?" Don picked up the note and smiled. He wrote back, "That's Nia, 'hunk-a-Nia' -- You'll be hearing a lot about her." Ben looked puzzled as he read the note. Don noticed and scratched a note to Ben.

"They call her, 'hunk-a Nia,' cuz most guys here have gotten a hunk of Nia," Ben read the note a couple of times trying to get what Don was talking about. Finally, he just gave Don a fake knowing look and got back to his work. He was an innocent abroad, clueless in the way of women and the world.

St. Margaret's was co-ed so Ben had grown up around many girls, but they had been like sisters. Of all the girls, he and his friends at the Home mostly hung out with Rosebud. Her real name was Rosemary but she hated how girly it sounded so she had been given the nickname Rosebud, which later became just, "Bud." She was like one of them and she could catch, pass and punt a football better than most of the guys. She wasn't afraid to block the plate no matter who was barreling into home, and she could dribble circles around all the guys. He thought back to Nia. Maybe she was like Rosebud and played football; maybe "hunk of," meant that guys had tackled her. However, there was also Rebecca. She was an only child and was in the same sixth grade class as Ben. Rebecca was a beauty. She and Ben became instant friends. Normally the kids at the home sat as family, but since Rebecca didn't have siblings she was assigned to sit with Ben and his brother and sister. Ben couldn't believe his good fortune. She brought up feelings in Ben that he could not decipher. Sometimes when they were together he stammered and fidgeted. Being with her was not like being with Rosebud, or any of the other girls. It was different. How? He couldn't say, but he knew that he liked it.

He filed the term, "hunk of," in his brain with the understanding that it obviously meant something at his school and as such, he needed to know about it. Ben did not intend to ask anybody -- he figured he would just observe and listen. The meaning would come to him.

Innocence was a virtue the nuns had worked hard to protect within all the children at the Home. As a result Ben had never been allowed to go to the parties of his school friends. Other than the outings to various charity events, his social life revolved around the activities of the Home. The nuns had created a sanctuary and a safety net for the children, and it had worked. Now Ben was swimming in the middle of a perfect storm where adolescence, surging hormones, and the freedom to explore had converged. At the Home, when adolescence arrived the newly emerged teens struggled with the boundaries that had been set and the requests for information on sex and sexuality became demands. The nun's thinking had been to address issues as they needed to be and not until then. So there were so many myths and misconceptions about hormones and anatomical configurations. The girls at the Home were able to get some idea of what was going on because of the nuns being females were able to clue them in, but the guys were for the most part in the dark.

Occasionally one of the boys would come back from visiting his family and tell of finding a Playboy magazine. He would try to describe the pictures he had seen which amounted to breast shots. In their innocence the boys imagined breasts as something with the consistency of firm water balloons, and wondered if girls could sleep on their stomachs. Nobody had an idea of the female form below the waist. None at all, not even the older guys, no matter how hard they pretended to have seen one – they were lying because the descriptions were so vague.

As Ben entered adolescence and began to have sexual dreams, whenever he got to the possibility of seeing a naked girl in his dreams, the image was distorted in that her body looked like his. This was because his brain had nothing to recall in regard to girls, other than in a clothed state. The nuns had done well in keeping his and the other's innocence intact even as Ben approached eighth grade. Innocence is the first loss, and Ben was innocent way beyond his time.

This was also a time of transitions. Some of his friends who were older than Ben began to leave the Home. Family members came to pick them up or they were sent to Boys Town in Nebraska to continue their education and go on to the next level. These were friends who had become brothers and sisters to Ben and now they were going away. All of a sudden his security was crumbling and he began to feel other emotions he had not felt before like . . . loss, unsettledness, and anxiety. The innocence of ever after was shattered. The Home was behind him, and now in California innocence was about to become a relative term.

CHAPTER 4

When he got home Ben quickly jumped in the shower. He stood there letting the water roll off hoping that his anxiety and unsettledness followed the water down the drain, but they hung on and his fear increased. Afterwards, he stood looking in his closet at the clothes the guys had given him in a type of catatonic stare. Although he had a limited selection, he couldn't make a choice. Numerous thoughts flew in and out of his mind. He considered calling Don and telling him that his Uncle had forbade him to go to the party. Ben knew he had the option to go or not to go, the nuns had taught him that people always have a choice. The idea was to make the right one. He wondered if going to the party was a good idea and almost talked himself out of going. What if someone wanted a "hunk-a," him? What if there was going to be a lot of "hunk-a," going on?

Ben made the decision to go. His sense of adventure trumped his fear. He was curious and thrilled. Out of the 815 kids at his school, he was one of the chosen. Ben put on the cords that looked the newest a long sleeved T-shirt and his tan vans. He walked over to his cousin Becky's mirror to give himself one final look-over, and then headed toward the door to wait on the curb for Don's parents to pick him up.

Various cars were lined up outside of Susie's house dropping off kids. Ben saw that Ken and Dennis were already there and talking to some of the cheerleaders. He looked around to see if he knew anybody else, then stepped out of the car with Don.

The party was being held in the den. The lights were low with strings of white Christmas lights draped overhead. Chairs were lined up against the walls and a stereo played music from the corner. The den also held a guest bedroom, but the door to that was closed. Before long, a crowd had gathered and started milling around.

After a while Susie called for everyone's attention and introduced the first event of the night; a game of "Knife and Fork." The idea was that a slow song would be played and as the kids danced, the girls would pass around a fork and the guys would pass around a knife. If the song stopped playing, whoever ended up with the fork and knife went in the guest bedroom for seven minutes.

Ben was standing along a wall taking it all in. He watched as each one of his friends ended up with the knife and went in the bedroom with various girls and came out smiling. The rest of the guys would hoot and give them a thumbs-up. He was busy trying to figure it out when a girl came over and asked him to dance. He didn't know it, but the guys had set it up. Ben walked with the girl to the middle of the room and joined the others as they danced. He felt the knife being passed to him just as the music stopped.

For a moment Ben didn't move. He looked around to see who had the fork. The girl he was dancing with held it up. She took his hand and led him into the room closed the door and sat on the bed. Ben stood by the door and looked at his watch. He had exactly six minutes and forty-eight second left to go. Out in the den the music had started up again and people were talking. The girl seemed to be waiting for Ben to get things going so he started making small talk. He was unsure of what this was all about, so he went to his "go to" tactic whenever he was in an uncomfortable place. He started telling jokes -- which he was excellent at. The girl was cracking up and laughing hard when somebody yelled out in the other room. "Time's up!"

Ben and the girl walked out with huge grins on their face. Don, Dennis, and Ken looked at them in disbelief and gave Ben a thumbs-up. Ben returned the gesture, then strutted over to them. Time would reveal later that they were faking it. Nobody was jumping on anybody, at least not in this group. Everyone was talking big; even about Nia. Nobody had yet gotten a hunk-a Nia.

He had come into town as an immigrant from the high desert of El Paso, Texas. Everything about him shouted, "kook," yet he had not only survived, he had won the middle school social sweepstakes in his first year. Crazy!

Ben was in Wonderland. It had been a banner year, a definite red-letter year. California was growing on him, he had loads of new friends, and he was cool. Now if he could only get his own room. Sleeping on the couch was getting old.

CHAPTER 5

St. Margaret's Home for Children had become Ben's home because his relatives could no longer care for him and his siblings. They had valiantly and with great generosity tried. However with growing families of their own and shrinking budgets, a decision was made that Ben and his siblings would be better together than to be separated. So they were placed in the care of the Sisters of Charity of the Incarnate Word rather than passed around to various foster homes.

Fifteen years had passed since Ben had first entered the Home. He remembered vividly the day that he arrived. A moth was slowly making its way up the curtain covering the window in the administration building. It continued its ascent as they sat in the living room waiting to be processed as the newest members of the Home. Ben respected and held moths in awe for their ability to forecast rain. It was his grandfather Nicolas who first gave him this bit of knowledge. "See a moth inside the house, expect rain within the hour," he'd say. Ben mentioned that rain was on its way to a nun sitting at the desk. She gave him a polite but condescending smile, and continued her work. After they had all been processed, and were departing to see the cottages that would be their home for the next eight years, a thunderclap shook the building and rain began to fall. Ben looked back at the moth and noticed the nun at the desk looking in disbelief at the wall clock.

Eight years later, in the summer of Ben's seventh grade, his best friend Rodrigo and he were walking over to the Administration building because Sister Florentine had said that Mrs. Grace had requested to see Ben. They were talking as they walked trying to figure out why he had been called there. His immediate thought was that he was in major trouble. But it would prove to be worst than that. Rodrigo sat on the steps while Ben went in to see what was up. Ben had learned from past experiences that these meetings were never good. The last time He had a meeting with Mrs. Grace, she made him dress up in a baby bear costume so that they could use him as a poster child to raise funds. But this time felt different. The premonitions he was feeling prophesied of difficult days ahead. Ben's intuition proved correct. Sitting in Mrs. Grace's office that day he was pelted with the news that he would be leaving the Home to go live with his relatives in California. Mrs. Grace told him that he would live in a big house and have a room to call his own.

Initially Ben was calm, but when the reality hit that he would be leaving in a matter of weeks, he erupted into a maelstrom of emotion and ran out of the building, frantically racing to the cotton fields seeking shelter in Rodrigo's and his secret place. He was swarmed by questions. "Who was this uncle?" "Why was he doing this?" "Didn't he know that this was my home?" "What about Rodrigo and Rebecca?" When he didn't show up for supper, Rodrigo went to their hideout and brought him back to the dining hall.

Later as he and Rodrigo lay in bed, Ben spilled the news to him in somber tones. Neither of them knew whether to celebrate or cry. They had been each other's constant companion and champion ever since they had met. They talked about running away, about Ben sneaking him into the trunk of the car. They talked of ideas and laid out plans to prevent this from happening, but then just laid there in silence. When the day came for Ben to leave, the nuns packed his one suitcase in the car and he obediently climbed into his uncle's car. Ben had the feeling you get when you're at the dentists sitting in the dental chair and the dentist says, "open up." You know what's coming, but you dutifully open your month. It's not quite surrender -- it's more a quiet resignation to the inevitable. Things had happened so fast that there wasn't time for a discharge ceremony which all of the kids who were leaving were given. It was like a tornado came in and whisked Ben away. There was no accounting for the eight years Ben had spent at the Home. All those years were simply packed away with the rest of his stuff in his suitcase. The number 18 which had identified all that was his would be given to another. Rebecca would forever remain a memory.

On that fateful day, Ben's uncle's car pulled out of the drive way and away from the only home Ben had known. All of a sudden, he heard someone calling, Ben turned around and saw that it was Rodrigo running hard after the car and waving a jacket that Ben had once loan him. He cried for his uncle to stop the car, but he refused and kept on driving. Rodrigo kept frantically running. Ben leaned over the back seat of the car and looked out the window to see Rodrigo slumped down on the road clutching the jacket to his chest. All he could do was slide down the back of the car seat and dejectedly stared at the road ahead of Him. One day he was running through the cotton fields of West Texas, and the next he was surrounded by the teens of the Orange Coast.

CHAPTER 6

B en was sitting reading, when there was a knock on the door. He walked over and opened the door to see a man waiting to be let in. At the same time, Ben's uncle came into the room. When he saw who it was, he let out a loud greeting with great affection. "Come in!" "Ben, this is your dad."

Ben followed the man and his uncle into the living room, where they sat in stilted silence. Finally his uncle shared how Ben and his siblings would be moving out and moving in with this man, their dad. He was told that the man lived in an apartment nearby and that they would finally all be together. Ben listened quietly and looked at the man with astonishment. There sitting across from him was his father. Right off, he noticed how quiet the man was. He hadn't spoken ten words since he had entered the house. The man was dressed in overalls worn by mechanics. He was wearing a faded baseball cap and sat looking down at his hands clasped together on his lap. All the while, Ben's uncle kept talking about what a great situation this was going to be for everyone. He wanted to tell his uncle to shut up so he could talk to his dad, but the many years of training on how to be respectful to adults kept him from interrupting his uncle.

When Ben's older brother and sister came home, they were clued in to the plans for the family to move in with the quiet man. In the end, they all figured it couldn't be any worse than what they were currently experiencing, and the idea of having their own place sounded appealing. That weekend the quiet man came to get them and take them to their new home.

At long last he finally belonged to somebody -- somebody who was his own flesh and blood. Someone he could call, "dad." Not only that, he and his brother and sister would no longer feel like intruders. They would have their own place with their own food. Never again would they feel guilty about getting a snack out of the fridge or the cupboards. Ben didn't care if he had to share a room with his brother he was ecstatic about not having to sleep on the couch.

The newly formed family arrived at their apartment, but it was not exactly what Ben had imagined. There were only two rooms, but four of them. He mentally did a room-sharing scenario and reasoned that his sister would get her own room. That left his brother, his dad and himself needing lodging. Ben figured that since he was the youngest, he would end up back on the couch. He was relieved to discover that the second room had a large walk-in closet, which the quiet man took for himself. That left the bedroom for him and his brother. Feeling greatly relieved, Ben gathered his stuff and settled in.

The apartment was located in a complex with large trees and lush lawns. After doing a reconnaissance of the area, Ben discovered that he was now within walking distance to the high school he would be attending in the fall, but further away from where Ken and Dennis lived. It didn't matter though. It was just distance.

The siblings had only been with the quiet man for six months when they began to notice that their dad drank . . . a lot. Ben's brother John decided he was not going to live in the apartment and eventually joined the Marines and moved out. When the quiet man began to be rude to Ben's sister, she moved out with a neighbor who had heard their dad's drunken episodes. It was now just Ben living with a man he had never known and who did not know him. Ben called his uncle and told him about how the quiet man was messing up and that his brother and sister had left, but his uncle only said that it would pass and that his dad would be fine. It wasn't, and it was going to get worse.

That summer Ben started his day by getting up before his dad. He'd grab a couple of Pop Tarts and leave the house, staying out until his dad had left for work and then return to enjoy the peace.

When the quiet man came home, he would sit and stare out of the window doodling on a notepad until it got dark. The only way that Ben knew he was still there was the red glow as he took a drag of his cigarette. There were never conversations between the two. It wasn't that Ben hadn't tried; there were many days when Ben would attempt small talk. There were even times when Ben would throw out jokes, all to no avail. Ben was so relieved when his dad left for the bars because that meant that he would have the apartment to himself until at least 2 AM when the bars closed and the quiet man would return.

This became the pattern of life for Ben. In time he began to stay out later and would spend as little time in the apartment as possible. Ben became an insomniac and dealt with the inability to sleep by embracing the night. Long after his dad had fallen into a drunken sleep, he quietly snuck out and would roam around the grounds of the apartment complex ingesting the stillness of the darkness and the star lit sky. Sometimes he would just run in an attempt to exhaust the adrenaline that fed his anxiety.

Amazingly, Ben was able to cover up all of this madness. None of his friends had any idea that he had stopped living with his uncle and now lived with his dad. Ben didn't mention it and displayed a calm and confident demeanor. He appeared carefree and freely joined in on whatever his friends had going.

When the guys showed up at his uncle's home to take Ben to the beach, they were told that Ben no longer lived there and were given directions to Ben's apartment. Don rang the doorbell and waited. Dennis and Ken were sitting in the car. Don was about to knock on the door when, it opened, he was greeted by Ben's dad.

The quiet man had two drunken stages. When he was in the funny drunk, he was hilarious. Such that if Ben could be assured that every time his dad got drunk, he would end up in a funny stage, he would keep him drunk and take him on the road as a comedian, serving as his manager.

The mad drunk was just that . . . mean, cruel, verbally abusive, and angry. Ben's dad would return from the bars in this stage, yelling and cursing and calling for Ben. He would turn on the bedroom lights and yank the covers off of Ben, then pull him off the bed, and berate him for hours.

That day though, his dad was being good-humored and gracious. When Don and Ben joined the guys in the car, Don said, "You should meet Ben's dad. He is a hoot and such a great guy."

Ben's friends noticed that he was always able to attend activities, parties and events. Where some parents would say no, people could count on Ben being there. As a result, his dad's reputation only improved. People thought that he had the greatest dad, and Ben agreed with them publicly. In his heart he knew how it really was, but he wasn't telling.

Ben's wish to not sleep on a couch had been granted sooner, but not in the manner he had expected. Ben had his own room, but not a home. He had a roommate, but not a father -- just the quiet man who only became animated and conversational when fueled by alcohol.

CHAPTER 7

High school freshman orientation is perhaps the most significant day on the calendar for the hormone infused senior guys. The most ambitious of them would get up early, drive over to the high school and position themselves where the new students would be signing up for classes. The shrewder among them would volunteer to be guides and assistants in showing the freshmen around and helping them with lockers. There was a point to this benevolent behavior, which was to have first access to the hot freshmen girls. There was no denying it. The girls from Ben's group were hot, and on the radar.

Dennis walked over to where Ben and the guys were standing in line with some of the girls. Two enterprising seniors came over to introduce themselves to the girls and offer their services, totally ignoring the guys. In a short time the upper class men had absconded with the best looking of the girls and left the rest to navigate the registration process and layout of the school by themselves.

When the girls eventually rejoined Ben and his friends at lunch, they were all giggles and astonished that they had been invited to a party at one of the senior's house.

"Are you guys going?" asked Ken.

Katy looked at him as if he were crazy . . . "of course!" The rest of the girls laughed and resumed their chatter about the upper class men, describing them as if they were gods. Don got up to leave.

"You sound like a bunch of chickens about to lay eggs." He motioned for the guys to follow him.

Susie walked over and snuggled up to Don. "Oh, relax, we told the guys that we would only come if we could bring you guys. They were cool with it,"

Just like that, the guys were going to be hanging with the big dogs.

Nobody was ready for what they were to meet with that weekend. They didn't even have a clue. The football game was uneventful due to the team getting creamed, but the environment was charged with energy of the band, the cheerleaders, and the crowd. Ben inhaled the night air and thought --- "this is good," then sauntered over to gaze at the blond cheerleader who had smiled at him in science class.

Later that night, Ken parked his car at the house where the girls said the party would be. People were standing around on the lawn and in the driveway. The guys walked through the crowd looking for the girls. Don and Dennis, who were big for their age, easily passed for older students. Ken and Ben felt self-conscious and definitely looked out of place. They tried to make themselves inconspicuous, but they were soon approached by a couple of giants who grabbed them by the collar.

"You boys lost?" growled one of them.

Ben was about to speak when he heard a sweet voice come from out of the crowd. "They're with us."

Katy and the girls had arrived just in time to prevent them from being launched into the stratosphere. The seniors dropped Ben and Ken and walked off. Don and Dennis who had been watching came over laughing.

"You guys should have seen your faces." "If you need to change your pants, the ladies can help you find a bathroom."

Parties during their middle school years had been mostly all show and big talk, like the knife and fork game, but not this party. The dimly lit room displayed silhouettes of the shenanigans occurring in the room. People were doing the couch mombo, the couples dancing looked like they had melted into each other, the alcohol was flowing, and students seemed to be willing to snort whatever Michelle was selling. Ben had heard that if she liked you, she gave free samples. The girl was a walking pharmacy.

After the party, Ben and Ken walked home without the rest of the group. Don and Dennis had convinced some girls that they were seniors and had disappeared with them, and neither of them knew where the girls had gone. Something had been lost that night. Something that Ben and his friends could not put words to, but it was gone and they knew it.

The group attended so many parties that it was hard to tell one from the other. Some of his friends began to drink, some began to smoke, and although Ben hated the taste of booze, he drank in part to be in, and partly to deal with the insanity of this phase in his life. His foundation was wearing away. Values that he had developed and cherished were put on hold. Worst of all, he was rapidly becoming apathetic and drawing deeper into himself. Nothing mattered, and at times Ben felt that he mattered to no one.

His pain was dealt with in two ways. He made jokes, or he lied. Both were coping strategies. He meant no harm. The problem was that because of his cheery countenance no one knew he needed help. Also, because Ben was so good at creating stories and lying about how good things were that he got himself believing his own lies. It was always a blow to him to come home and to be confronted with the truth.

As the year wore on, he became reckless. At night Ben walked in the areas of town that were known to be dangerous. Sometimes he followed the quiet man to the bars and watched from a distance as people greeted him and welcomed him into the room. He wondered what would happen if he rushed into the bar and thrashed it. What if he confronted his dad and told him what his drinking was doing to him? Then he realized that the quiet man and himself were both using the same medicine to heal the pain. Maybe they were running from the same thing. Maybe they were more alike than they knew. Ben shivered at the thought and quickly erased it from his mind. He was nothing like the man. Biologically there was a connection, but there was a great chasm between his heart and the heart of the quiet man.

CHAPTER 8

One morning as Ben bent down to tie his shoe he noticed an envelope sticking out of a military footlocker that his dad kept in the walk-in closet bedroom. The envelope had an official look and an air of importance to it. Ben walked into the closet and lifted the lid of the locker and pulled it out. It was really more of a packet and held several documents. He held it in his hands and discovered that it had been mailed to his uncle and was from the State of Texas Child Welfare and Protective Services Department. Although he knew his dad was at work, Ben walked into the living room to make sure the door was locked. He sat down at the kitchen table and began reading through the documents. Ben looked down at the signature at the bottom of the first page and was shocked. Mrs. Grace, the social worker at the Home, had prepared the package. The letter read:

Dear Mr. Storm,

We are excited to be partnering with you in the transition of your nephews and nieces, the Storm children, from

St. Margaret's Home for Children, to your home. We have taken great care to ensure that this transition is done well and with minimal emotional turmoil for the children.

Please note that although you are the children's legal guardian, the State of California will serve as the supervising agency. As such, the children are legally Wards of the State of California. If this arrangement becomes unacceptable and troubled, the State will step in to assist you and the children.

You will continue to receive the monthly financial support and medical, dental, and vision coverage for the children as long as they are in your care. In addition, a social worker will be assigned to this case. Please expect a call from the Child Protective Services Department within the next two weeks. Also, if the children leave your care, you must contact the Child Protective Services immediately, and surrender any funds that you may have in this account.

Enclosed in this package are various documents that will assist you in learning how to access resources, important contact phone numbers, and support services. You will also find vouchers for the first two months to help you get the children settled and make any necessary purchases. I will be in contact with you early next week.

Sincerely,

Evelyn Grace. LCSW

Ben quickly rifled through the rest of the documents. He found the medical vouchers and everything else that Mrs. Grace said would be in the package. What he didn't find was the name and number of his new social worker. He filed through the paper again to find the cover letter so that he could get Mrs. Grace's number and quickly wrote it down. He also found the number to the main office of Child Protective Services. Then Ben gathered the documents and carefully placed them back in the envelope. He walked back to the closet and placed it back in the footlocker exactly as he had found it, and walked out of the apartment.

He walked for blocks until he arrived at the old abandoned house that had become his refuge. Once inside, he climbed the rickety staircase and sat in what used to be a library. He felt like a pawn and that his life was being played out like some giant chess game. It all made sense to him now. His uncle and aunt didn't want him. They had just set up this elaborate plan so that they could then turn him and his siblings over to their dad. Ben had no idea that in the past his dad had attempted to gain custody of them but had been unsuccessful.

He felt resentment rising up within. The feelings of betrayal were resurrected which ignited the anger that he had attempted to suppress for the past year. It now began to seep out from within him and then to boil over. Ben jumped up and added to holes in the wall that had been caused by the kicks of the many who had also expressed their pain in this place --- some, who like him, had kicked out in frustration and a sense of helplessness.

The room grew gradually darker as Ben paced. He thought about calling Mrs. Grace and telling her that her grand plan for his siblings and him, had blown up; that it was a giant cruel joke. He wanted her to know that she had been tricked and lied to. Ben lay down on the faded carpet and watched the moon come up from behind the oak trees that surrounded the house. He woke up in the morning still in the library of the house cold and hungry, but with a plan.

CHAPTER 9

Sometimes it's just a matter of where you are at a given time that serves as an impetus to try another way. Such was the morning of June 5. Ben was shooting hoops with some friends in a part of the city where he had never been. The upscale houses loomed all around him with perfectly manicured lawns. Expensive cars lined the sidewalks and rested in driveways. It was the most beautiful place Ben had seen.

While they were playing, one of Ben's new friends, Mike, shared with the group about how he now had enough money to buy his girlfriend the huge stuffed toy tiger she had wanted. He also displayed a new watch, a couple of rings and a stack of tickets to Disneyland.

Mike looked at his friend Jon, who winked at him like they had some sort of secret between them, which they did. Jon's dad had been the contractor for the entire development. As a result, he had a key that opened the door to every house in the development so that he could gain access into the house while it was being built. Now that the development was finished, the key was no longer needed and he had placed it on the key rung in his office and forgotten about it, but Jon had not.

It was this key that had provided Mike with all his new found wealth. They had been breaking into homes in the area for the past year. When they asked Ben if he wanted to come along on their next heist, he readily agreed without a second thought. He had nothing to lose and he might end up with some things that he would never have access to otherwise.

The plan was simple --- go to the door, ring the doorbell. If someone answers, ask if they've seen a black cocker spaniel. If no one answers, they would then go around to the backdoor and enter the house. It was surreal the way that Mike and Jon would enter the home, do a five minute ransack and head out the door. Ben stood in the living room acting as a look out. When they got to the third house, every innate survival instinct within Ben began to go off. He nervously went to the sliding glass door and opened it so that they could all make a quick escape.

They had pushed their luck. The family had returned while Mike and Jon were still upstairs. Ben called to them to run but it was too late. The family was already at the door. Ben slipped out through the glass door and ran for his life. He had run two blocks when he stopped to see if just by chance, the guys had made it out. Five minutes passed and he didn't see or hear the guys. Ben decided to wait a few more minutes. When it was evident that they would not be coming, he turned around and headed back to the house.

There were two police cars parked in the driveway. Ben could hear the dispatcher talking from within the cars. For some unexplainable reason, he walked up to the door and rang the bell. A gruff looking man opened the door. Ben could see the guys sitting on a couch with the policeman standing over them, while they took notes.

"Yes?" asked the man.

Ben didn't speak for a moment and then said, "I was with them."

The men looked at Ben, and then back at Jon and Mike. "Do you two know this boy?"

Jon was about to say that he did, when Mike slightly nudged his knee and gave him a look that said, 'shut-up!' "Naw," said Mike.

There was nothing to connect Ben to the scene other than his strange confession. Unlike the guys who had multiple watches on their wrists and rings on several fingers, Ben didn't have any merchandise. One of the cops came over and pulled him aside. " You say you were with these two?" he asked.

"Yes sir, I was." replied Ben.

The cop's partner came over to where Ben was being questioned and said, "It was either him, or somebody else. There are three sets of footprints in the backyard."

With that evidence, Ben was handcuffed and walked over to join his friends in the police car and then sped off to the local Police Station for processing.

He couldn't sleep. The room was cold, the voices coming in from the hallway and the constant opening and closing of doors made it hard to fall asleep. In the morning, Ben laid in bed covered by only the thin sheet. He turned his head to the side and slowly opened his eyes. It hadn't been a dream. He had spent the night in a jail. The bars of the cell seemed to mock him for his stupidity. "You were free with no connection to this mess, and you had to turn yourself in. "Chump!"

When the quiet man came to get him, he merely signed the documents and motioned for Ben to follow him. Neither of them spoke as they were driven back to the apartment. The stench of shame permeated the car. The quiet man felt shame that his son would have to stoop to stealing to access goods, and Ben sat drenched in the shame of compromise, and the abdication of all that he knew was good, true, and right.

The rest of the summer, Ben kept mostly to himself. He played summer league baseball with Ken and the guys, but he couldn't get past the choices he had made. As a result he carried the load of guilt and wondered if the guys were embarrassed to be seen with him.

There are better ways to begin your second year of high school. Ben began his with the misadventures of Mike, Jon, and Ben being broadcast all over the school. Mike turned it into a big joke, and blew it off. Jon the rich boy got grounded for the summer and had his car taken away. Other than that he was over it except that Mike and Jon ended up on probation for the next two years. The police determined that Ben had been a tag along and after reviewing his records from the Home, decided to have a court officer do periodic home visits. Nobody had a clue that he was living illegally with the quiet man, or that he was a ward of the State of California. That would have completely changed everything.

During one of those visits that the court official made to Ben's apartment, his dad was caught in one of his mean drunk stages. As Ben was climbing the stairs to the apartment, he heard yelling and cussing. The door was open and the quiet man was demanding that the court officer leave immediately. The man was walking down the stairs and saw Ben. He motioned for Ben to walk with him to his car. Once there, the court officer asked Ben how often his dad was like this. Ben hesitated and ran scenarios through his mind. What if he told the truth and the man reported it to Social Service? Then he thought if he did, he might be able to connect with his new social worker that would make his uncle take him back and away from his dad. His worst fear was that he would be placed in foster home with people he had no connection to or knew. Finally, Ben answered.

"My dad's job is really stressful and he goes on a binge every couple of months. He'll be all right. We're doing good -- really."

The court officer seemed to be scanning Ben to determine if he was telling the truth. So when Ben's relaxed and unconcerned manner suggested that he was, the man pulled a business card out of his pocket and handed it to Ben.

"If things change and you need help, call me at that number."

Ben waited until the man drove off. He knew he wouldn't be able to go into the apartment until his dad passed out, which would probably be within the next two hours, so he walked over to the next apartment complex and did his homework in the laundry room. It was business as usual.

CHAPTER 10

D on sat in his car honking for Ben to come down so they could leave for the beach. Ben looked like he hadn't slept for a week. By now he had clued Don in that his dad was an alcoholic.

He unlocked the door and let Ben in. "Crazy night?"

Ben threw his gear in the backseat. "Yeah, my old man was in some rage over some women. He finally passed out at 5 in the morning."

The car pulled away from the curb and they headed off to the beach.

"You can crash on the beach, then why don't you stay at my place tonight," Don said.

Sleep came easy at the beach. The monotonous rhythm of the waves breaking on the shore was the ultimate lullaby. Ben fell into a deep sleep. His subconscious mind took him back; back to a happier time -- back to the days at the home surrounded by his friends, the nuns and the wide-open spaces.

In his dream, he was walking into the cottage where he had lived. The cottages had big porches that led into a living room. At one end of the room was a kitchenette and at the other a library. Leading out from the living room on both sides were long hallways with dorm rooms on either sides. At the end of the hall stood a door leading to the outside. He saw his bed with a wooden chair at the end of it, and his dresser decorated with his treasures. In his closet hung his school clothes and two coats. Everything else was folded neatly in drawers. The dresser unit also served as divider to his best friend Rodrigo's space.

On the walls of the dorm, a colorful picture of Jesus was mounted depicting Jesus surrounded by children. At times it was a great source of comfort for Ben. Other times it caused frustration when he struggled with the rigidity of religion. God at times seemed so distant and unapproachable and at other times he longed to climb into the picture and stand among the other children close to Jesus' side.

The vividness of the dream drew Ben so deeply into it, he started smiling, talking, and gesturing in his sleep. Don watched and listened with fascination. When Ben abruptly awoke and bolted up, Don jumped back.

"What was that about?" "Man, you were dreaming hard" a startled Don, exclaimed.

Ben forlornly looked around. He was still at the beach. He was still in California, and he still had to go home to the quiet man.

"I was having the best dream. I dreamt I was back at the place where I grew up. The dinner bell had rung and I was about to race my best friend to the chow hall," Ben replied.

They lay back down on their towels and retreated into personal spaces.

"Where's your mom?" Don quietly asked. Immediately he felt foolish for asking. He quickly retracted his question. "I was just wondering, you don't need to answer that."

Ben got up and walked to the shoreline. He stood looking out over the water, then waded and swam out until the ocean had enveloped him, tossing him to and fro amongst its waves the way that a washing machine does to dirty clothes. Finally the waves cast him upon the shore, exhausted. He picked himself up and rejoined Don on the beach. Don started to offer up an apology, but Ben cut him off.

"I know very little about her," Ben began.

"She took off a few weeks after I was born. No one really knows why. I've heard some stories from my relatives, but they're all one sided. All that I know about her is that she was diagnosed with Tuberculosis right after I was born, and ended up in a hospital here in California. According to the story, she met a man and ran off to make another life for herself. I have no idea what she looks like. For the most part, I've given her the benefit of the doubt, since I've never heard the whole story."

Ben pulled his T-shirt on, shook the sand off his towel, and gathered his gear.

"We should go."

Don had resurrected a question that had been pushed way back into the recesses of Ben's mind. Now as they drove home, the question had resurfaced and was doing laps around his brain. How was his mother able to bypass her maternal instinct? How was she able to leave her children, why did she leave him?

"Let's get Ken and Dennis and go get some burgers. We can all crash at my house tonight," Don offered.

Sitting at A's Burgers that night felt good. It was like old times. It seemed that the summer incident had never mattered to the guys, other than to be concerned for him. It was Ben who had chosen to cast himself as a social leper, and isolate himself. He casually mentioned to his friends that he would probably be moving back in with his aunt and uncle.

The guys joked and laughed until dawn. As the tiredness of the day crept in, they began to fall asleep; except Ben. He was savoring the peace and safety of the room. It had been a long time since Ben had prayed. It had been even longer since he had been to church. His direct line to heaven seemed to have been disconnected with nowhere to forward his calls. He recalled the picture of Jesus and the children that had hung in his dorm room at the Home. If there was ever a time when he needed to be held close, it was now.

CHAPTER 11

He had always been intuitive. It was his gift. So when the impression to pack his belongings and leave hit him, Ben listened. He went to the footlocker in his dad's closet-room and pulled out the package prepared by Mrs. Grace. Carefully, he found the cover letter, pulled it out and placed the rest of the pack back in the envelope. Ben pulled the suitcase from under his bed and quickly filled it with all that he owned, turned out the light, locked the door, and headed off to his uncle and aunt's home. On the way, he stopped at the post office and made three copies of the letter. The original and two of the copies went into his suitcase. The other he placed in his shirt pocket.

The time to launch the plan that emerged as he sat in the library of the old house had come. He gently touched the letter folded up in his shirt pocket. Ben now had his passport to where or what, he wasn't sure, but he knew he would not be coming back to the apartment or the ranting of the angry, but quiet man.

Walking to his relative's house gave Ben a chance to rehearse what he was going to say. He wasn't sure whether to come on strong and tell them that he was on to them, or to be mellow and do a common sense approach. One minute he was all fire and thunder, and the next he was for peace and calm. As he got closer to the house however, He decided that he would take a very matter of fact approach, just the facts.

Ben knocked loudly and waited. A neighbor noticed Ben at the door and called out,

"They should be getting back from vacation today. Anything I can help you with?"

He walked over to where the man was standing. "I'm their nephew." He stuck out his hand and introduced himself. "Name's Ben."

The man took Ben's hand. "I'm Tom. I've been watching their place while they've been gone. I expect them here 'bout dinnertime. You're welcome to wait for them at my place."

Ben thanked the man and walked back to his suitcase. "I'll just wait here," he said. "I appreciate your offer, sir."

A few minutes after the street lights came on, a car came up the street and pulled into the drive way. The driver's side window slowly rolled down.

"Ben?" "What are you doing here?"

Ben's uncle stepped out of the car and walked over to where Ben was sitting.

"Everything all right?" The man eyed Ben suspiciously. He noticed the suitcase and the resolved look in Ben's eye. This was not at all what he planned to come home to. He had planned to return to his quiet house, in this quiet neighborhood. To be greeted by a somber adolescent sitting in his drive way had not been part of his itinerary.

Ben stood up and handed him a copy of the letter.

"I found this in my dad's stuff. I'm sure you're familiar with everything it says . . . especially the part about how you're my legal guardian, and that in case you weren't able to fulfill that position, you were supposed to call Mrs. Grace. It doesn't say anything about us living with our dad, and now I know why."

"You also need to know that John and Sandi have left. John joined the Marines and Sandi has moved away. It's just been my dad and me for over a year."

There was a look of concern in his uncle's eyes. Ben had never seen a scared adult male, but he was looking at one. The man walked slowly back to the car. He seemed to be consulting with his wife. When he returned to Ben, he said, "You'll have to sleep on the couch until we can find a bunk bed to put in Max's room."

A breeze began causing the trees to sway. It felt like something was being ushered in. Something fresh. He thought it strange how he had began to notice trees. Ben watched them for a minute, and then walked into the house. It wasn't the ideal situation, but it would have to do for now. He knew the quiet man would be showing up soon, and he had a plan to deal with that too. No longer would Ben be at the mercy or whim of others. He would be flexible like the palm trees; yet strong and stable like the stately oaks that grew around the deserted mansion in which the plan had come to him.

When he moved in, the most difficult thing to deal with at his uncle's house was the tension. The times at the dinner table were the worst. Everyone sat there in silence with bowed heads. It was the proverbial, 'walking on eggshells,' scenario. The family stepped carefully around Ben like they were afraid of him. Faux etiquette and politeness were extended to him. This went on for a couple of days before Ben decided to break the spell. He started telling jokes. At first there where only muffled giggles, and small smiles. After his third joke though, everyone lost it and food went spraying across the table as his relatives let loose with gut splitting laughter.

Laughter had negotiated a contract of sorts. Ben only needed a place to stay. At least that's what he was telling himself. In the morning, he was gone long before anyone was awake. He put on his best clothes and went out looking for a job.

CHAPTER 12

"Aren't you ever going to come party with us?" Katy pleaded with Ben to show up at her house for her birthday. It had been awhile since he had been to anybody's party. Ben had gotten tired of the routine and the taste of booze. He didn't want to get dragged back into the scene.

"What if we go to Knollwood's and get a burger or something?" Ben offered. "We could go to the beach afterwards."

The rest of the conversation did not go well. Ben knew he was blowing his chance with Katy. Of all the girls he had met, she was the one that had not only caught his eye, but the one who seemed to have her stuff together. She had class. Was it a veneer? He didn't know anymore, and he was not biting. Ben turned down her invitation and hung up the phone.

There was talk going around school that Ben had become a monk, although he still hung out with the guys and played sports. On weekends he would hitchhike to the beach and walk for hours along the shore and then sit and watch the waves roll in. Eventually he started taking his sleeping bag with him and crashed for the night in the lifeguard towers. He remembered reading a quote by the author, Isak Dinesen who wrote; "the cure for everything is salt water; sweat, tears, or the sea."

For Ben it had been a mixture of all three. Right now, it was the sea that was providing the cure.

While walking one weekend, he met some surfers who had called out and asked for the time. Shortly after that day, he became a part of their group and was soon sharing waves with them. Ben was sure he had found what he had been looking for. He now had brothers, a lifestyle, and the salt water. He became the ultimate earth child. His hair grew past his shoulders, and he was introduced to avocado, cucumber and sprout sandwiches on organic whole wheat bread. He embraced nature as a mother, fully enjoying her embrace as he lay on the warm sand.

Early on in his junior year, Ben's friends at school noticed a change. He seemed to be more at peace. Serene even. Another change was that Ben began cutting school more. He frequently ditched classes for the morning surf. Although his uncle mentioned that the school had called, neither of them gave it much thought until the truant officer made a house call. That put a stop to the ditching and relegated surfing to the weekend.

Normally fall in California brings sunny days, well-formed swells, and some occasionally insane Santa Ana winds. That year, something was off. There was the sunshine, the epic beach conditions and even the Santa Ana winds tore through the region on a number of occasions, but the waves were noticeably and painfully absent.

Sitting around the fire rings, his friends were bemoaning the lack of waves, and the flat spell they were enduring. Initially, what had attracted Ben to this bunch of guys was their authenticity. He had never been around a group of guys who were able to share thoughts and emotions the way they did -- and, they weren't even drunk!

That night though, they resorted to what most of his friends did to deal or just to chill. Huge doobies filled the night air with their pungent odor, bringing a sweet comfort to the group. Ben felt conflicted about his feelings of condemnation and judgment running through his heart. He wanted to yell out: "What are you guys doing?" "This is how you deal with disappointment?"

His Nirvana was a sham. Ben reasoned that when push came to shove, and pain comes into ones life, the response is self-medication in some manner. He concluded that if that's how it was, he might as well profit socially from it. He heard that there was a party and decided to go. At least there, he had status, and Katy might be there.

It was like he had never left. He looked around the room; it looked like a re-run of an old movie. He was about to leave when he saw Katy staggering as she attempted to dance. All of a sudden she started dry heaving, which was quickly followed by volumes of the previous night's linguine noodles. They splattered the crowd and rolled down on her chest. People scrambled to get out of range. Katy then toppled over and lay in the center of the room. Two guys came over to check on her and then each grabbed a leg and an arm and carried her out of the room.

Ben remembered hearing how this is what Katy did. Drink, pass out, and then guys would take advantage of her, but not tonight. He followed the guys out and watched as they counted to three and then chucked her behind a bush to sober up. He waited until they left and then went over to turn Katy on her stomach so that if she threw up again, she wouldn't choke on her vomit; and left her there.

Disgust. There was nothing else you could call it. Every pore on his body oozed disgust. How could he have just left her there? Ben looked deeply at his reflection in the mirror.

"You're sick, dude, and so are your friends. "

As painful as the realization was, it also served as Ben's wake-up call. He wanted desperately to find his way back to who he knew he was; to do what he knew was right. Yet he found himself always winding up where he had been before. He'd been going in circles without making any progress. Then like a lighting bolt, a directive came to him. Ben was sure he had heard a voice. He didn't bother to look around because he knew no one else was home. The voice had come from within.

"Work the plan."

That was it. That's all he heard. In the morning, he would initiate phase two of the plan.

CHAPTER 13

He had just barely opened the front door when Ben saw his dad coming up the road. He could tell that the quiet man was drunk. Ben quickly shut the door and ran to the back door. He walked through the backyard and looked over the fence. He couldn't see his dad, but soon heard the pounding and yelling as his dad called for his uncle. Ben waited until he heard the door open and close, then he ran down the street toward the nearby strip mall where he had filled out several applications. He would leave the explaining to his uncle.

Ben walked from business to business until he came to Graziano's Restaurant. He opened the door and walked into a darkened dining area. He could hear the clatter of pots and pans, and was pleasantly engulfed by a variety of epicurean essences. His nose went on overload. As if on cue, his stomach began to growl with the pangs of hunger. He closed his eyes and took another deep breath. Ben walked toward the source of the sounds and the scents and saw a chef mixing magic into a pot on the stove, and energetically singing along with Luciano Pavaretti to The Marriage of Figaro, playing from his boom box.

Although he had called out to the chef several times, the man had not heard him. So Ben walked into the kitchen and tapped the man on the shoulder.

"COSA!" Yelled out the chef, as his spoon went flying into the air. He reached for his huge butcher knife and spun around to face his attacker.

Ben froze. He felt a small amount of fluid slide down one of his legs. His right cheek was twitching, and no matter how he tried to speak, he couldn't. Finally the chef put the knife down. In a thick Italian accent, he said,

"I could have killed you! Why are you sneaking into my restaurant?"

"I'm here about the dishwashing job," a wide-eyed Ben stammered.

The chef did not appear convinced. He walked over to a table and picked up a stack of papers.

"What's your name?"

"Ben, Ben Storm, sir."

"Aw, Ben, do you have experience washing dishes?"

The chef's changed demeanor helped Ben relax. He released the tension in his shoulders, and rubbed his sweaty palms together.

"Yes, sir. I've been washing dishes since I was six." This was a true statement because at the home, once a child could reach the top of the sink, they were added to the kitchen duty rotation list. Ben had spent many mornings rinsing dishes, cup, pots, pans, and loading them into the huge dishwasher.

"Well, then, Mr. Ben, you're hired. You begin tomorrow at 5:00 PM." The chef reached out his hand, "I'm Lee, welcome to Graziano's.

Ben walked to the door in a daze. He was an employed man. He was going to have his own money. All sorts of thoughts were flying through his mind when Lee called out to him.

"By the way, Ben, the job also includes delivering pizza. Do you have a car?"

A car. Now that was going to be a problem. Ben not only was minus a car, he was minus a driver's license. He hadn't even taken the driver's training class. At sixteen and a half, he was one of the youngest members of his class and the only one without a license. He slowly turned around.

"I don't have a car."

Ben was expecting that statement to end his employment.

"No problem," said Lee. "You can drive mine on deliveries. See you tomorrow."

As a matter of survival, of self-preservation, he kept the rest of the information about his lack of a license to himself, and walked out the door. He rationalized that he would make up for that lie by being the best dishwasher in town, and a pizza delivery boy who always arrived with the pizza steaming hot.

What mattered was that now Ben was a member of the American work force. He declared his independence from everything and everybody. From now on, if he was going to make it, it was up to him alone. Hope surged in Ben's heart. He could not put into words the feeling he now had over having been hired. It was something like, gratitude to the 1,000th power.

When Ben returned to his uncle's house he saw that the quiet man was still there. He stopped, watched, and waited.

"Why doesn't he just go?" Ben thought. "Just go away, and leave me alone."

Surprisingly, that's exactly what happened. The quiet man just left. He took to the road and drifted from one place to another. That day at his uncle's house was the last time Ben saw his dad alive.

Ben didn't know how to feel about the quiet man. Although he carried emotional wounds from their encounters, it was difficult for him to acknowledge the anger. He vacillated between feelings of pity for the man, and feelings of guilt over his inability to develop a relationship with the quiet man and come to know him as his dad.

CHAPTER 14

T he liquid Amber trees that were scattered around the high school were the only ones to turn colors and lose their leaves. The fall of Ben's senior year, they put on a spectacular show. It reminded him of the autumns he had spent at the Home. He remembered the cottonwoods and the poplar trees going from green to shades of yellows and orange. He remembered gathering the huge, dried out tumbleweeds and shaping them into walls to build forts, and battling the wasps as they made last minute attempts to enclose their larvae in paper nests before the cold came. On the coast, other than the wild grasses, which went yellow early on in June, the color green dominated the land. One had to be extra vigilant to catch the changing of the seasons in Southern California. That's how it was with Ben. The changes that had been occurring within him had been constant but like the changing of the Southern California seasons, subtle.

Two significant events occurred at the start of Ben's senior year. One of them was going to set events in motion that would forever alter the course of his life. The other was a change that had come over Katy.

The first thing that Ben noticed as he ran into Katy in the hallways at school was that she looked incredible. Gone were the lifeless eyes, the pale skin, and the downer vibe that had clothed her and hovered over her for the past couple of years. She looked like the girl he had met in middle school, just older.

"You look great." He said.

Katy gave Ben a shy smile. "Where are you headed?"

"Kline's class. Psych." Then he quickly added, "but I know where I'm going."

Katy turned Ben around. "It's this way, I have that class too."

Call it déjà vu, a flashback, or whatever. In that moment they were back at middle school before the insanity of high school had begun, even before the quiet man. The important thing was that Ben had found Katy. Here she was again, still smelling like coconuts and with that smile. Katy had found something. Something deep. It was within her, but radiated out.

After class Ben walked Katy home. Although they had not seen each other for months, they walked in silence. When they arrived at Katy's house, they lingered at the doorway making small talk. Finally Katy opened the front door and was about to step inside when she turned and walked back to Ben.

"Ben, I have so much to tell you. What if we go to the beach this weekend?"

"I have to work."

Too late -- Katy's face spoke volumes. In her mind she interpreted Ben's statement to mean that Ben was still seeing her for who she had been; the loose party girl. She walked back to the door and stepped in looking out at Ben.

"Maybe another time then --- check your schedule and let me know."

With that, she closed the door. Ben stared at the closed door for a while. He looked up and saw Katy standing at her window looking down at him. He was feeling something; something that was buzzing through him like voltage. Ben stood back to get a better look at Katy, who had now opened her window, "call me if you change your mind."

The second event involved some of his other friends. Lilly, Dave, Dennis, and Michelle, the "walking pharmacy girl." They had started going to church. Not only that, they were hosting a Bible study during lunch right on campus. There were at least 50 students sitting in a circle talking about Jesus like he was just some guy on campus. It was a weird assortment of ex and current stoners, preps, jocks, grits, surfers, and cheerleaders. Ben watched from a distance with intrigue. The fact that many in the group were some of his ex-partying buddies made him curious. Olivia though drew his attention more than the rest. What was a Goth chick doing in that group?

While others dressed to impress, Olivia dressed out of a sense of ideology. Her obsidian black hair framed a pale face. The way she applied make up to her eyes added to her exotic and striking appearance. She had come into Christianity, but had brought her Goth ways along with her. It was a classic juxtaposition. Regardless, she was a quiet but faithful attendee at the noonday Bible study; a priestess clothed in black, but now calling herself a child of the day.

Ben was intrigued. At the Home, Ben had been immersed into all things God. He had started serving the Mass when he was seven years old, dutifully working hard to memorize the Latin responses to the prayers and statements spoken by the priest. Ben had served so many Masses, always volunteering for the High, the Holy Days of Obligation, Requiem Masses, and Masses for the dead. He had been taught that he would get extra plenary indulgences that were like get-out-of-jail-free cards that would get him out of Purgatory quicker. Ben figured he was covered.

He couldn't deny that there were times when he had brushes with the spiritual that he could not explain; like the time he was walking to Midnight Mass on Christmas Eve. That winter night as he was on his way to serve the Mass, Ben looked up to see the night sky as he had never seen it before. Although the Geminid meteor showers had peaked earlier in the month, on this Christmas Eve, a few stragglers remained and blazed as they passed by. Ben couldn't help but think of the star, the Christmas star. It had been the gift he had cherished most that year.

Another time Ben was sitting in the pews with the rest of the faithful reading from his Missal. He looked up and began to gaze at the various icons of the saints, the stained glass windows, and the ceramic plaques depicting the Stations of the Cross. Numerous white candles lit up the room, and incense wafted from the censures that the altar boys were holding. When he got to the statue of Joseph the humble carpenter, the earthly father of Jesus, Ben dropped his Missal in amazement. He was sure Joseph was looking directly at him with warmth and affection; a father's affection, one that Ben had never known or felt, but hungered for. After the Mass, he waited until most of the people had left and cautiously walked over to the statue. He reached out to touch its hand, and quickly pulled it back. The statue was ice cold. How he had felt so much warmth emanating from it? Yet he had felt a definite connection.

Those were just two of several incidents that were shrouded in mystery and had left Ben with a sense of awe. Now all of that was in the past. He had gone from being devout, to being skeptical, to becoming an agnostic. Still, he watched the "Jesus Freaks" with fascination, but not so much that it caused him to accept their invitations to their Bible study or to church.

CHAPTER 15

Max was sitting on the couch when Ben got home from school. "Sup, Max the Mighty?"

The boy looked up and Ben noticed a massive black eye radiating from his face.

"What the hell! What happened Max?"

"I-I-I-I-I go-oo-o-t hiii-t w-i-it-t-th a b-b-b-a-a-l-l, " he said.

Ben went into the kitchen and pulled out a bag of frozen peas from the fridge. He gently placed it on Max's eye and held him. His cousin had been hit hard, and it wasn't by any ball. Ben tried to get Max to tell him the truth, but the boy kept insisting it had happened during recess. He was deep in thought when Max's older sister Becky arrived home and walked over to where the guys were sitting. The bag of frozen peas that Ben was holding on Max's eye immediately set her off.

"Those idiots!" She yelled. "It was Jack and the guys, right?"

Max tried to deny it but Becky knew she was right. The group had been making fun of her brother since the beginning of the school year. Even though they were in fourth grade, they somehow managed to sneak over to where the primary grades had recess and torment the younger kids. Max was their favorite target due to his stuttering and timid manner.

In the time that he had been living with his cousins, he had developed a close relationship with them. They had become siblings, having adopted each other. It wasn't through legal means, but it was binding -- heart to heart.

Max's parents' jobs had them on the road a lot, and Ben filled in. He brought them pizzas and pasta dishes from his job and made sure they did their homework. It helped that Becky was in middle school and was able to help with Max and with the house. When it was just the three of them, it was like being a family. When their parents returned things would get awkward. Max would come to Ben for help with his schoolwork instead of going to his parents. After a while, Ben began to notice that his Aunt would quickly tell Max to come to her, that she would help. It was like she resented how close the kids and Ben where.

Ben had Max hold the frozen peas and called Becky into the next room.

"Who's Jack?"

The next day Ben called Becky's school and said that she would be coming to school late due to an important appointment.

He and Becky walked to Max's Elementary School and waited as the buses pulled up to drop the kids off. Becky pointed Jack and the guys out, Ben walked over to them talking aloud to himself,

"These kooks are in need of a 'how to be nice,' lesson."

The boys were about to walk toward the playground when Ben confronted them.

"Excuse me gentlemen. I believe you are wanted in the office. Follow me."

The students looked at Ben then at each other. "Are you a teacher?"

"Yeah, I guess I am." "I'm going to be your teacher. I'm here to tell you that you are not to be seen messin' with anybody younger than you; especially my cousin Max. Now, normally, I would take matters into my own hands, but then I would be a bully like you kooks. So we're going to go a different route. Either way, from this day on, you will treat Max as if he were your ruler. Got it? Good. Shall we go?"

The terrified group of boys followed Ben into the Principal's office. He stopped at the desk and began to share his story with the Principal's secretary.

"So I'm wondering if you could call my little cousin down so the Principal can see for himself."

Ben heard a voice coming from behind him. It was a voice so low that it sounded more like a growl and like it belonged to King Kong. He turned around to see a giant standing behind him. The giant had huge feet, huge hands, a unibrow, and was not at all pleased by what he had heard.

"Thank you Ben. We'll take it from here."

Becky and Ben glanced over their shoulder as if to make sure the boys were going to be dealt with, and saw the boys walking slowly into King Kong's lair.

Becky was livid as they walked home. "Why are people so cruel? Max is nice to everybody. You'd think it would get him friends, but people treat him like a freak just because he stutters."

Ben didn't have an answer . . . at least not one that didn't sound like a cliché. He put his arm around her as she sobbed quietly. When they got home, Becky went into her room and shut the door. Even when justice prevails, the pain continues. She knew that Max would be dealing with this issue for as long as people like Jack and his chumps were in the world.

That night as Max and Ben lay in bed, Max said in the most perfect iambic pentameter, "I am so glad you are in our family."

Ben bolted up. "Max!" "Was that you?" "How did you do that?"

Max looked at Ben wide-eyed. "I-I-I-I-I d-d-d-o-o-o-n-n-n-t k-k-k-n-n-no-o--ow."

Ben jumped out of bed and walked over to Max's. "Try it again." "Say what you said before, take your time." The boy opened his mouth and let loose with a string of staccato timed sentences streaming out of his mouth like it was a machine gun. Ben ruffled Max's hair.

"No big --- if you did it once, you'll do it again. That was amazing!"

Becky and Max loved Ben. He was the best surrogate big brother anyone ever had. The crazy thing was that the closer they all got, the more Ben's uncle resented it. It became a source of contention that manifested itself by Ben's uncle acting out on him in passive aggressive ways.

Later, walking down the hallway to his room, Ben heard his aunt and uncle arguing in their bedroom. He stopped at the door and heard his uncle say that he had to go; that it was time for him to go live with another of the relatives.

Listening to music as he drifted to sleep, Ben decided that he agreed with his uncle. It was time for him to go. The next morning before he had a chance to say anything, Ben's uncle asked Ben to go for a ride with him. It occurred to Ben that his uncle was doing the cat thing. He was going to drive Ben around and around then drop him off in some strange part of the city so that Ben could not find his way back home. There were many times when Ben cracked himself up, a coping device he resorted to when the great "suck" was coming. This was one of them.

They drove on for miles. Ben could see that his uncle was thinking hard. The veins in the man's face bulged and sweat forming on his upper lip. He felt sorry for him. Maybe he should just tell him that he had heard their conversation and to chill. Just as his uncle was about to speak, Ben spoke out.

" One of my friend's family has asked me to move in with them. I figured since it's my senior year, it would be a good idea."

Ben's uncle tried to act nonchalant and played like there was no way he would allow it. Then with great drama, he reluctantly agreed. Ben acted like his uncle had just done him a huge favor and thanked the man.

In the morning, Ben put his life savings into a canvas bag and stuffed it in his suitcase with his clothes. He wrote a note to Becky and Max explaining what was going on and promised to visit often and to keep the deliveries of pizza and pasta coming. Before going to work, he bought a sleeping bag and a flashlight.

Washing dishes that night gave Ben time to think. Among the many thoughts going through his head was that he had paid big for not giving his boss the full info on his driving license. Some nights he would get all caught up on the dishes only to get called off on a pizza delivery. By the time he returned, there were tall stacks of dishes, glasses, pots, and pans waiting for him. He shook it off as a type of penance. Often times he would not leave the restaurant until after one in the morning. The positive thing was that it had given him plenty of time to plan his next steps. Ben had known that he couldn't stay at his relatives forever. It had been getting tense and awkward for a long time. He knew that if he told the guys that they would take him in, but that's not what he wanted. He had a job, he had money, and he would be all right.

After work Ben walked to an orange orchard that he had passed often on the way to Ken's house. He had noticed that the grasses had grown tall and that the oranges went unpicked as if the orchard had been abandoned. Walking deep into the orchard he found a spot where the grass grew the tallest and would provide him with a good hiding place, and a soft place to lay his sleeping bag. After looking around he found a tree whose branches where almost touching the ground creating a space where he could crawl in.

"Perfect," he thought.

Ben crept in, unzipped his sleeping bag and lay down looking up at the stars through the branches, while the sweet scent of orange blossoms floated in the night air. He would live here; at least for the time being. It was close to work and school. Ben figured he could keep some of his clothes in his gym locker and take showers at the school gym if he went to the early practice sessions. This was it. No more accusations, and no more jealousy.

CHAPTER 16

The problem with living outdoors is that the world wakes up so early. Birds go off at the first sign of daylight. The mockingbirds don't even wait, they've been singing all night. Next come the cars. Even from his place in the middle of the orchard, Ben could hear the early risers racing to get on the freeway. He ducked his head into his sleeping bag and attempted get a few more Zs, but it was useless. The cacophony continued.

Ben dragged himself out of his sleeping bag, pulled his clothes on, packed his sleeping bag, hid all of his belongings under layers of grass, and headed off to the boys locker room. After his shower, he walked over to the vending machines, grabbed a bag of Doritos and a coke, and then headed toward his first period class.

A week had passed since Ben had been living in the orange orchard. Everything was going smoothly and he loved it. He sat in class looking like every other kid who had woken up in a house, went through the morning routine, and now sat in rows around him. There was no sign that marked him as a kid living in an orchard. That's exactly how he wanted it. For all anyone knew, Ben was still living with his relatives.

A panicked thought shot through his mind. What if the guys came looking for him at his uncles like they had before when he had moved in with the quiet man? Ben was running several scenarios in his mind when his name was called.

"Mr. Storm?"

Ben's head shot up.

Mr. Kline, his psych teacher walked over to the blackboard. "Please identify the three aspects of the human personality according to Freud, and which of these is most active in your life currently,"

"The id, the ego, and the superego. The id is unconscious and contains everything that is inherited, everything that is present at birth, and the instincts. The ego is conscious and controls the demands of the id and of the instincts, becoming aware of stimuli, and serving as a connection between the id and the outside world. In addition, the ego responds to stimulation by either adaptation or flight, regulates activity, and strives to achieve pleasure and avoid displeasure. The superego, which manages the demands of the id, is responsible for the limitation of satisfactions and represents the influence of others, such as parents, teachers, and role models, as well as the impact of racial, societal, and cultural traditions," explained Ben.

Mr. Kline and the class were stunned. The teacher walked over to Ben's desk to see if he had read his statement, only to find that all that Ben had on his desk was a #2 pencil. He had memorized the entire reading.

" Excellent, Mr. Storm." "Now which one shows up predominately in your classmates and yourself?"

Ben shifted in his seat and did a quick mental review. "I'm not thinking Freud paid much attention to adolescent development except in psychosexual areas. Bottom-line, Freud believed and I quote, 'that adolescence was a time of massive behavioral, social, and emotional changes; he also thought that there were relationships between the physiological and psychological changes that influence our self-image. In people our age, the physiological changes are mostly related to emotional changes, especially an increase in negative emotions, such as moodiness, anxiety, loathing, tension and other forms of adolescent behavior.' So I would have to go with id.

"Give that man a cookie!" exclaimed Mr. Kline.

The majority of Ben's teachers were frustrated by him. His teachers liked him, but dreaded having him in their class because of his reputation for his ability to disrupt a class in a manner that there was no way of bringing it back to order. There was the time he intentionally drank a quart of milk and had his lactose intolerance kick in during class. The janitors not only had to prop open the windows, but they also had to bring in a huge industrial fan.

His teachers knew he had the stuff; why he didn't cash in on it drove them nuts. At best, Ben would produce "C-/D" quality work, then show moments of high intellect like in Kline's psychology class. Although Father Stephen, the nuns at the Home, and at Our Lady of the Valley had done an excellent job of providing him with foundational tools and knowledge, Ben had been wasting that gift for the past four years. His senior year of high school had started the same as the previous four with a cumulative GPA of 1.75. He just didn't care, and the majority of his classes bored him to the bone. It also didn't help that he had frequently missed his first period class to go surfing. School for Ben was a time to be with his friends, and because he had to be there; that was it, but it was not how it used to be.

Where one starts and what words are first spoken, can matter in significant ways. These words can be detrimental, or they can go a long way in insulating and inoculating one for the journey ahead. The outcome of this can result in what one has to offer to the world. When Ben entered the Home, it was as if he had been re-booted. His first start had not been so great. The words that he had heard were not life giving. Lucky for him, a new script had been written and it contained a whole new set of words. Among the first new set of life-giving words spoken to Ben, came the words from Father Stephen who was the priest in residence when he arrived at the Children's Home. Father Stephen had the dual duties of serving at the local Catholic Church and with the children at the Home. The man was like Solomon. He had a vast knowledge of all things flora and fauna, of engineering and mechanics. He loved art and music. His study was full of books and artifacts from around the world. Going to his house was like going to the museum. It was he who bestowed upon each of the kids at the Home the title: "Gentleman and Lady Scholars." They believed him. Ben believed him, and it showed up in his behavior, his academics, and his ever-present sense of hope.

A crotchety old coot named Father Hyatt, took Father Stephen's place a couple of years before Ben would be discharged from the Home. The kids called him Scrooge. He was caustic and cranky and appeared to dislike children. He would yell at the altar boys when they did not perfectly perform their duty during the Mass. It was during his tenure that the altar boys started acting out in response to his constant corrections and reproach. They would take the left over wine used in the service and the unconsecrated wavers used for communion and run off among the trees in the fields and lament their misfortune. Ben went to the next wafer and wine party with strong misgivings. While the guys were in the midst of the event, one of them took a hefty swig of the wine just after he had crammed a handful of wafers in his mouth. Ben watched with horror as he eyes began to bulge and his face began to turn blue. Finally one of the older boys whacked him hard on the back producing a steam of wafers and wine followed by a huge gasp for air. The boy lay on the ground gulping in air, while he wet his pants.

After that event the parties stopped. The altar boys decided that judgment had come down and that God had given them a sign of his disapproval. The wine and wafer parties became a thing of the past and those elements representative of the body and blood of Christ, became what they had always been taught they were -- holy. Fear is a powerful thing and may be connected to reverence. Ben had known better, but at that stage in his life, he was more concerned about coolness than catechism. As he walked away he felt a great relief, but he also felt repentant.

The wine and wafer episode changed the altar boys. From that point on, all tried to give Father Hyatt the benefit of the doubt. They started going over to his residence like they had with Father Stephen. But it was no use. Ben and the guys realized they would never change him. So they just took him as he was and tried their best to please him. Still there were times when no matter how he tried to be stern, now and then people saw glimmers of kindness. And no matter how he attempted to keep the Mass solemn and serious, when he chanted during the highest of Masses, The Requiem Mass, he sounded like the cowardly lion begging for courage. Even the nuns struggled to muffle their laughter. Why he was sent to the home was a mystery. Perhaps his heart had grown cold, or maybe it had been wounded in the same way that the inner city nuns experienced. He may have been sent to the Home to heal. Whatever the case, after awhile the children avoided him as much as possible and he interacted with them only when it was required. Ben realized that life was teaching them some hard lessons, but he had no idea of the lessons that lay before him. Father Hyatt might have come into his life as a harbinger of a lesson he would have to learn -- that no matter how hard one tries, some relationships are just not going to happen.

All of that goodness, healthiness, and industry that the nuns and Father Stephen had placed in Ben's heart were now lying dormant under layers and layers of apathy, anger, and angst. He was classic Id, in desperate need of Ego.

By the end of the class Ben reasoned that since his friends did not care for his uncle, they wouldn't be looking for him there. He would have his friends pick him up at work, or meet them at their homes. His secret was safe.

CHAPTER 17

Lightning flashed all around. Ben bolted from a sound sleep. Every clash of thunder shook his body and made his ears ring. To avoid death by electrocution, he flattened himself so close to the ground that he and the earth became one. The storm continued on with great force for the next hour. After the thunder and lightning, the sky opened up and let loose a torrent of water that lasted about fifteen minutes. Ben and the sleeping bag he was laying in were immediately soaked. The rain then turned into a soft drizzle and continued on with no sign of abating.

He looked at his watch. 2:00 AM. Ben looked at the mess that the rain had created. He knew that 6AM was right around the corner and he would have to set off to school. He wondered if he had enough time to walk to the Laundromat at the apartment building where he used to live. It would be the perfect place to wait out the rain because he could sleep there while his clothes and sleeping bag were in the dryer.

Out of nowhere he was blindsided by a wave of negativism. Part of him wanted to lay back down in defeat. Maybe he was trying to make something happen that just was not going to be. How long could he really keep his situation secret and sustainable? Ben was enjoying the pity party when it was crashed by the voice; the same voice he had heard in the old mansion and the one that he had heard at his uncle's house.

"Work the plan. You've come too far. Get up, and get going!"

Startled, Ben jumped to his feet, the hairs on his arms and on the back of his neck stood rigid in fear. This was the third time he had heard the voice and every time he had obeyed it, he had made progress. He made the decision to go to the Laundromat, and quickly gathered his stuff and headed off to the apartment complex.

The drizzle remained constant as if to mock his attempt to continue to fight for independence, but Ben kept walking. When he arrived at the Laundromat, he quietly open the door, opened his school bag, tore off the cardboard cover of his notebook and wrote, "Out of Order," then placed it on the window of the door. He turned off the lights, locked the door, peeled off his clothes, placed them in the dryer along with his sleeping bag, and changed into jeans and a t-shirt.

Ben crawled under a table, and sat with his back against the wall, and looked at his watch. It had taken him thirty minutes to walk to the apartments. Outside, the rain continued. He began to freak about getting to school in the rain. Then Ben remembered that a school bus stopped at the apartments, which solved the transportation problem. What would he do with his stuff? He couldn't drag it around school all day. That would raise all kinds of questions. Ben got up and walked around the room. He noticed a row of cabinets along one of the walls and went over to inspect them. The cabinets were labeled and had laundry and cleaning supplies in them except one of them. He leaned down to open it and looked inside. It was packed with old clothes and rags. After rummaging through the pile, he realized that he could hide his stuff in the back of the cabinet and cover it up, then come back to get it after school. Having solved his dilemmas, he sat back under the table and fell asleep.

In the morning, Ben woke up with the worst stiff neck of his life. He had fallen asleep sitting up, so his head had been drooping with his chin at his chest for all those hours. He was about to crawl out from under the table when he heard the doorknob jiggle. Ben froze and held his breath. The person on the other side of the door was being very insistent.

"Sheesh! Can't you read?" Muttered Ben.

At last, the person walked away, exclaiming loudly their frustration at having walked all this way with their heavy laundry and in the middle of the miserable rain. Ben waited until he felt sure that it was safe to come out from under the table. When it was obvious that he could, he bolted out, washed and brushed his teeth in the sink, grabbed his jacket and his school bag, and ran quickly to the bus stop. There were about eight kids standing around waiting for the bus, one of them was Olivia. Ben was about to do an about face when she noticed him.

"Ben!" Olivia called out. She walked over to him. "What are you doing here?"

Unable to come up with a quick explanation he bought himself some time by making small talk.

"Hey!" "I didn't know you took this bus," he calmly replied. I was walking in this crappy rain when I remembered the bus stopped here. I used to live in the apartments over there."

It worked. They were soon talking about current events amongst their friends and school when the bus pulled up.

"Come on sit with me," invited Olivia, "You can have the window."

Ben didn't recognize the rest of the students on the bus. Most of them were freshman and sophomores who were yet to get their license. Olivia was looking at her notes for a test she was going to have that day. He leaned over to see what she studying.

"Civics?" "Whose class do you have?"

Olivia answered without looking up. "Henshaw's"

"Why are you riding the bus?" "I thought you drove."

" I do drive, when I have a car to drive. My brothers and I have one car to share between us. Most of the time though, I walk to school. I don't mind, it gives me time to prep for the circus that is our school."

Ben liked her. Behind all that black and counter-culturalism, was a very cool chick. He had heard that Goths were moody, depressive, and cynics who worshipped the devil. From what he was picking up from Olivia, none of those traits fit. She emanated a strong sense of peace. He had not met anyone who seemed to be more comfortable with them self than her. She had flashlight eyes; eyes that shone so bright like they were powered by super energizer batteries. When she laughed, it came from deep within; loud and unbridled. People would hear the laugh, turn around, and be puzzled to see that it came from a petite Goth girl. And she liked it that way. He was captivated.

"Do you want to meet for lunch?" He asked.

Olivia looked up from her notes. "I have lunch with my friends. You're welcome to join us."

"You mean with the group on the center lawn?" Ben squirmed in his seat. All of sudden things had gotten uncomfortable.

She put her notebook back in her bag. "Yeah. We eat and talk about God things." "You know a lot of the kids, I think you'll like it."

The bus pulled up to the curb and students began filtering out. Ben didn't know how to respond. If he declined, she would think he was anti-God, if he accepted, he knew he would ultimately end up challenging the group on their beliefs which might turn her off. When Ben didn't respond to her invitation, Olivia stood up.

"Think about it."

By lunchtime, the rain had stopped. Ben was looking elsewhere and rounding a corner when he collided into Olivia. It was a full-head-on crash that sent what each of them had been carrying flying and knocked them down in such a way that Ben ended up on top of her.

He jumped up and extended his hand.

"Are you all right?"

"You're supposed to slow down at blind corners." "Remember?" Olivia glared.

She took Ben's hand and tried to be serious, but the bad puppy look on Ben's face elicited that great laugh of hers.

"I'm fine," she said at last. She looked down at the scattered books and papers. Ben looked down and realized he was still holding her hand.

"Uh, Ben?" "I need my hand so I can pick up my stuff."

Ben quickly let go of her hand. "I'll get it. I'm sorry if I've hurt you," he said. "I'll make sure to slow down at that corner from now on."

"Or, at least let people know you're coming." Olivia walked off to join her group, "Honk, or something!"

When the last bell rang, Ben went to the apartment complex. There were two people folding clothes at the tables. He stood outside of the Laundromat and waited for them to leave. When they left Ben quickly gathered his belongings and headed to the orange orchard and to his living space. Although the ground was damp, it was dry enough for him to sleep on and he began to set up camp. He opened a can of peaches, some Vienna sausages and began to eat. Ben had weathered a storm, literally. He had handled what nature had thrown at him. He had shown himself to be resourceful. He was a survivor.

CHAPTER 18

A new kid had started working with Ben at Graziano's. Ben had seen him at the group that met at the Bible Study during lunch. Dave was quiet, incredibly polite, yet had a cool vibe going on. He and Ben hit it off right away. One night while they were at Dave's house rehearsing a Beatles tune, they got to talking about mutual friends and their experiences at school. Dave mentioned that he had gone out with Katy during middle school and talked about how he wished they were still an item. He went on about how awesome she was and how she always smelled so great. Ben had a flashback moment as memories of the time he'd spent with Katy were resurrected by what Dave was talking about. He bit his tongue and kept his comments to himself. There was no need to let on that she had also caught his eye.

"Do you know Olivia?" asked Ben.

"Not too well. She started attending our group last spring. We all thought she was mocking us being Goth and all, but she wasn't. She's a feisty one --I know that. She doesn't take any crap, and you'll always know where you stand with her. I guess I would say, she's genuine and . . . and hot. Why"

Ben shifted uncomfortably. "Nothing, but you're right. She does stand out sitting with you guys. I was just wondering."

The tape popped out of the tape deck that served as a reminder that it was getting late. Dave began gathering the sheet music, placed the guitars in their cases and called it a wrap. With the music of, "And I Love Her," playing in his head, Ben began the walk back to his pad.

When he arrived at the orchard, Ben hesitated before he walked to his tree. Somebody had been here. Recently. He noticed that the tall grass was flattened that led to his spot. Ben had always made it a point to conceal the path when he left and when he arrived. He decided to approach his spot from the rear so that he would not be detected. Carefully and quietly, Ben moved closer to where he slept. He stopped and listened for a few minutes. He threw a few fallen oranges toward his tree. Nothing. Finally, he gathered the courage to turn on his flashlight. With every bit of courage he had within him, Ben let out a Banshee yell and charged at his tree. Two birds bolted out of the tree and straight at Ben who threw up his hands to shield his face. He lay on the grass with his heart beating like a drum machine. When he had gathered himself he crawled inside, shone his flashlight around and discovered that somebody had gone through his stuff. The place was in shambles, but it didn't look like anything was missing. He quickly walked over to the next tree where he had stashed his money and found that it was all there.

Regardless, Ben felt violated. Several scenarios flashed through his mind as he considered his options. None of them were palatable to him. He was not going to cave in and go back to his uncle's. He would just have to move and find another place. What he knew for sure was that he could not stay here -- not even for the night.

Ben gathered his stuff and again made a trip to the apartment complex, and settled in at a different Laundromat than he had been before. No matter of how he attempted to calm himself his mind continued to race -- sleep would not be something that he would be experiencing to any degree on this night.

That next day he ditched school and began to scout out other living spaces. Ben knew it had to be in the same vicinity so that he would be close to school and work. All that day Ben went from location to location without any success. As evening came, he went back to the Laundromat where he had hidden his stuff, and thought. He seemed to be out of options. Despite all of his searching he had not found a location that would serve him as well as the orchard had. Depression and anxiety were beginning to set in. He felt hopeless and helpless. Ben ended up sleeping in the Laundromat again.

At work, he put on his public, everything is awesome, best day ever face. Outwardly, he was energetic and productive, but a cloud of uncertainty hovered over him. Ben was grateful when a pizza delivery required his attention. It allowed him to pull himself away from the constant ruminating over his predicament.

As Ben drove he continued to scout out possible living locations. He considered couch surfing with his friends but realized that it would put him in a dependent situation like the one he had been in at his uncle's house. He had hated the awkwardness of feeling like nothing there was his, not even the food. So that was not an option. If he had a car he could sleep in it, but he didn't. Then it hit him. An idea floated into his mind. He realized that he was always the last one to leave the restaurant. He could crash there. Lee never showed up before 8 o clock in the morning and Ben would be long gone by then. It would work for now, but it was not a long-term solution. He knew he would have to keep looking.

Still, the fact that he had a safe place to stay for a while, gave Ben renewed hope. He returned from his delivery genuinely energized. The rest of the night he took his time washing the dishes and delivering pizzas so that he would be certain that he would be the one closing the restaurant. During one of his pizza runs, Ben swung by the apartment complex and picked up his stuff and then hid it by the dumpster in the back of the restaurant. He would figure out a better place to stash it all in the morning, which included him ditching the suitcase and buying a backpack.

With the turn of the knob on the front door, and a flip of the switch of the neon light advertising the valley's best pizza, Ben walked to the back door to retrieve his belongings and then settled in for some desperately needed sleep. For the moment, Ben was still free and confident that his destiny was his to decide. He set his alarm clock for 6AM and drifted off to sleep.

When the clock hit 6AM, the radio blared out, Ben quickly reached out and tagged the off button. He maneuvered his way out of the booth where he had been sleeping, ran to the customer bathroom and got ready for school. Afterwards, he hid his belongings deep in the food pantry, went to the back door leading to the alley and cracked it open so he could see if any deliverymen were around. When he was sure no one would see him, he took off toward school.

Later as Ben was walking to class, a sense of something he could not explain hit him. Ben felt compelled to drop by his uncle's house. The feelings clung to him so persistently, and threaten to drain him of life if he did not comply. The feelings were so compelling that Ben was afraid not to give in to its demand. There was nothing he could do but obey.

Approached his uncle's neighborhood, there was a loud honk, and then a screeching of tires. Ben looked up wide-eyed. Inside the car Ken, Dennis, and Don were beside themselves with laughter.

"Watch where you're walking kook!" Don leaned out of the car, "get in, we're going to "A's".

Ben thought quickly, "Hang on, I gotta stop by the house and get something."

"Hop in," we'll give you a ride, called back Don.

Ben coolly climbed into the car hoping that his relatives weren't home. When they arrived, Ben calmly walked to the door and reached into his pocket like he was reaching for his keys. There were several business cards wedged into the door jam, and a couple of serious looking door-hangers dangling on the knob. He pulled all of the items off the door and walked back to the car.

"I forgot my keys. I'll be right back." Ben walked to the gate and went into the backyard. He found the garden spade that he had used to pry the sliding glass door open whenever the house was locked, and let himself in. The house was dark and vacant. It looked like nobody had lived there for quite some time. Standing in what use to be his and Max's room, Ben glanced at the business cards and saw that they were from the Child Protection Agency and belonged to a caseworker named Dante Wells. The door-hangers strewn about on the floor in the living room were between eight and six months old -- one threatened foreclosure. Ben continued walking through the house and then walked out of the door and out of his past.

"Guess I don't need to worry about any Case Workers snooping around, or anybody else for that matter." He mused.

He closed the sliding glass door behind him, threw the cards and notices on the ground and went to join the guys in the car. Although he had a massive sense of relief he also felt the most alone he had ever felt. It really was just him, by himself in the world. Maybe that's why the feeling to come to the house had been so strong. Was it a warning – a notice that he was playing for keeps, or was it so that Ben would respond and see that although a significant option had been taken away from him, a bigger significant concern had been removed from his life? All he had to do now was not draw any unnecessary attention and he would be fine. Ben climbed into the car and drove away with his friends.

At A's burgers, Ben announced that everything was on him. The guys didn't waste anytime ordering massive amounts of food and sodas.

"What's the occasion money bags?" asked Don between bites of his burger.

Lifting his cup of Dr. Pepper, Ben said, "Me, I'm the occasion -- a toast to me, the only free man in the city."

CHAPTER 19

Although Ben had a place to crash while he looked for a more permanent place, he felt unsettled. Because of this he was not sleeping well. Every noise during the night and the early morning startled him. He became hyper vigilant. Ben knew he had to get back to the sort of place he had in the orchard, away from any possibility of being discovered. He worried that he would be exposed as homeless and turned over to some foster home. The worrying served to provide him with the motivation to stay disciplined and cautious, but it also kept him in a state of constant tension that led to exhaustion. He was constantly on.

That night at the restaurant Dave's parents came in for dinner. They had been coming in for a while and had grown fond of Ben. Mrs. Menner would kid Ben about them adopting him. At first, it made Ben nervous because he wondered if she knew he was homeless. After a while though, he would just laugh it off. But it did make him think.

He watched as Dave brought his parents their food and noticed how they treated each other. There was such warmth between them. It was something he had never experienced and he had a feeling that he probably would not be any good at doing the family thing. He turned away and distracted himself by heading toward the sink and the ever-present stack of dishes clamoring for his attention.

At the end of the shift, his boss came back to the restaurant for a meeting with his suppliers. Ben slowed down on his dish washing so that he would still be the last one to leave, but the meeting kept going. Eventually, there was nothing more he could do. He took his time card and clocked out waving at Lee as he walked past the group.

"Thanks, Ben. See you tomorrow." Lee said.

Ben closed the door behind him.

"Now what?" "What if the meeting turns into one of their poker games?" They'll be here all night!"

He stood there trying to figure out where to go, and then started walking without a destination in mind. He circled back to see if Lee had left, but they were still at it. Ben peeked through the blinds and had his main concern confirmed. They were playing poker. He realized that he would not be spending the night here and knocked on the door so he could get his backpack.

"Ben!" "What are you doing back?" Lee said as he let Ben in.

"I need my school book. It's in the back," Ben replied.

He walked to the pantry and pulled out his backpack and set it by the backdoor and propped it open. Ben grabbed his book and walked back into the dining area and toward the door.

"Thanks, see you later," he calmly said as he passed the men.

Ben quickly ran to the back of the store. He quietly opened the door, reached for his backpack, and then gingerly closed the door. It was now past 1AM. He knew he had to find a place close to school so he would have time to take a shower, and headed off in that direction. He was careful to avoid being seen, especially by the police.

When he arrived on campus, Ben considered his options. He first thought the bushes in front of the Library might work, but when he checked it out, the ground was soaked. Next, he walked over to the Driver's training trailer and look underneath. There was plenty of room for him to slide under, but he dismissed this location too. Then it hit him -- the baseball dugouts! That would work. He walked over and stepped down and looked around. It was far enough from the classrooms so that it would look like he had walked to school if anyone saw him. He settled into one and covered himself with his sleeping bag.

Something was wrong, really wrong. Ben lay motionless, barely breathing. He could feel that someone or something was in the dugout, but the total darkness hid whatever or whoever it was. When he could no longer stand it, he grabbed the backpack and launched himself out of the dugout, dragging his sleeping bag behind him, running for his life. When he had distanced himself from the danger, he sat panting partly from exhaustion, mostly from fear.

It was no use looking for another place to sleep. The sun was beginning to send rays of light from behind the foothills. What he did need was a place to hide his gear. Ben decided to stash it in the bushes next to the Wood Shop classroom. He knew that area was never watered and that hardly anyone had a class there. He was on his way there when he heard some voices. Or he thought he had. In reality it was only the wind that had picked up and was wailing through the corridors. Ben didn't wait around. He took off running to the shop.

The campus was abuzz with the news of a dead guy being found in one of the baseball dugouts. People were freaked. When Ben heard about it he was alone in the guy's locker room. The news shook him to his core. For the first time since he had hit the road, he felt afraid.

He had always felt secure and safe. Now all of that had changed. Ben had taken to the streets because he had felt it was his only chance to make it. Since he had left the Children's Home, he had not met an adult he could trust. Ben had been on the streets for six months, yet had managed to stay healthy, well fed, and productive in school -- and now this.

He was deep in thought when Olivia walked up.

"Did you hear about the stiff in the dugout?" She asked as she sat next to him. "We were just in there the other day, creeps me out!"

Ben nodded, but he wasn't in a mood to talk. He stood up. "I have to go, he muttered," and walked away

"Nice seeing you too, Ben," she called. "I'm glad we had this chat."

During class Ben ran various scenarios in an attempt to see which one of his friends might be open to him spending a few nights at their house, but then just as quickly he shoved the thought out of his head. Ben understood that the dead guy could have been him. Regardless, he was resolved to be his own man, in his own way. He would find a place.

Ben concluded that the poker game in the restaurant had been a fluke. The card games were few and far apart. For now, he could continue to sleep there. There was no need to panic. He could take his time. What he did need to do was get a copy of the key for the restaurant. Ben also needed to chill and engulf himself in a huge container of salt water. The ocean would do.

When the bell rang he raced over to where he had hidden his stuff. Everything looked just as he had left it. He would come back later to get his gear. Ben walked over to where Don and Ken were having lunch and sat down next to them.

"Whose car is my wetsuit in?"

"That would be me. I also have your board," Don said. "Ditching?"

"Naw, thinking about going after school. You guys wanna come?" "I'll buy burgers afterwards," offered Ben.

Ken walked over to dump his trash. "I'm in." "Nothing but ankle-snappers breaking, but could be fun."

Don shoved the rest of his sandwich into his mouth, wadded up his lunch bag, and launched a three pointer, which bounced off the concrete wall and landed in the can. "I'll pick you guys up in front of the school."

CHAPTER 20

There were times when Ben would have dinner at one of his friend's house. While the food was being passed around he'd listen to the small talk, which was so soothing, and endearing that he found himself feeling ripped off and wondering why it couldn't be him. What had he done to anger God, the Universe, Karma, or whoever it was that resulted in him being sentenced to life without a loving family such as this?

Other times he'd be at a different friend's house at dinnertime and experience the direct opposite – at this table, emotions ranged from everyone sitting in awkward silence and picking at the food, to explosive argumentation which always ended with someone leaving the table in tears. At these times Ben would leave the house thanking the same powers that had ripped him off, for sparing him from the possibility of being born into such a family.

One place he loved hanging out at though was Dave's. In the time he had been hanging out with the family, he had never experienced any weirdness – plus, Mrs. Menner was an amazing cook. Dave knew that any time his mom was going to serve flank steak with mushrooms, Ben would definitely want to be there. Dave's mom's cooking ranked up there with the best. That night Ben was served more than the delicious steak dinner. He was offered a home. Eventually, he would look back on this night and wonder how it had all transpired.

Later, lying in the booth at Graziano's, he carefully evaluated Dave's offer. It seemed so win-win to him, yet his recent experiences with depending on others, raised a cautious concern. He decided that he would wait on making a decision.

This had all come about, because unbeknown to Ben -- Dave had mentioned to his family that he had a suspicion that Ben might be couch surfing. He wasn't sure why, but on several occasions Dave had seen Ben heading in the opposite direction from where his relatives lived as he was leaving work to go home.

Ben was still mulling the Menner's offer over as he walked to class the next day.

"Hey!" Ben turned around to see Olivia walking up to him.

"Where've you been?" "Did you get the note I put in your locker?" She asked.

"Yeah, I saw it. Sorry for not getting back to you. I've been working a lot and with gymnastic practice, it's been school, or work."

Olivia walked beside him in silence. Ben knew what was coming. Even though he had rehearsed what to say in several different ways, he still felt awkward telling her that he didn't have any interest in attending her youth group. Ben knew that many his friends like; Katy, Dennis, Lilly and the rest, would be there, but he wasn't ready to open that door yet. He was about to respond to her note when he had a huge insight. Maybe, he could finally get Olivia to go out with him if he agreed to go with her.

During the noon lunch hour, he made his pitch. "Tomorrow's when you guys have your meeting, right?" "You know, the youth group thing?"

She looked up and gave Ben a look that asked, "What did you say?"

He was about to say something lame, like, "uh, nothing."

He wanted to go out with her badly! So he repeated himself and added, "I don't have to work -- I'd like to come."

She wasn't sure if he was playing with her or if was serious, so Olivia calmly said -- "excellent." "I'll pick you at your house."

"You don't have to, I'll get a ride from Dennis and the guys 7PM, right?"

Ben felt a sense of loathing toward himself. He was a scheming, slimy slug using the thing that was most precious to her – her faith to get a date. Any minute now he expected to be turned into a pile of ashes from the effects of a lightning bolt sent from the Ultimate Judge and he deserved it. He almost did the right thing, but instead rationalized that he was in too deep.

Olivia couldn't put her finger on it but something was off. She decided to let it go. Things would reveal themselves, they always did. Right now, it was all good. Ben was coming to youth group.

While his friends eagerly entered the room, Ben hesitated. Through the open door he could see that the room was packed. He began to walk back to the car, when there she was. Ben decided to come clean. After a brief pause, he confessed.

"Olivia I told you I would come tonight because I thought I would have a better shot at getting you to go out with me." He waited. Ben fully expected chastisement, condemnation, or for her to walk away and with her, any possibility of getting closer.

"Why wasn't she saying anything?" "*Go ahead*, torch me," he thought.

However, that night, the lightening and the fire did not come, nor were caustic words expressed. She simply took Ben's arm and led him into the room where they settled in among their friends to hear about a grace like no other, spoken by a man who looked more like Fred Flintstone than a powerful prophet of God.

The man spoke about the ability to be free, to live as a son, but not just any son . . . a son of God. Most of this Ben had heard before. The parts that he grasped onto were the part about living free, no games, no masks, and no wax. The other was the son thing. To a kid who had never belonged to anybody, this concept connected. He had always understood the Son of God thing to refer to only Jesus. Fred Flintstone was saying that anyone could be a son of God. When the man invited the students to find out more about the process, he stood up and made his way to the front.

All over the room gasps of surprise were clearly audible. It was obviously a joke, Ben was messing with the man the way he would mess with his teachers. Everyone clearly expected Ben to go into his routine. Instead, he stood quietly while the man extended his invitation to others. No one else responded – it was the preacher and Ben up front and a room full of students who were riveted to what was occurring before their eyes. Dennis and the gang were sitting with their heads in their hands praying that Ben was legit. Olivia watched with hopeful anticipation.

It was Ben who spoke first. "How do I become a son?"

The man was a bit taken back by Ben's directness, but he quickly recovered and was genuinely intrigued by the young man who stood before him. The conversation that ensued took place as if Ben and the preacher were the only ones in the room. When the preacher was done explaining the pathway to Ben, he asked him if he wanted to pray. Ben nodded his head. The man addressed the students and asked everyone to bow their heads and began to pray over Ben – and then it was over.

It wasn't until Ben walked back to where Olivia and his friends were sitting that people began to get up and mill around the room. He wasn't sure why his friends were hugging him and patting him on the back, but Ben knew that something big had happened in his life – something significant that had nothing to do with religion, something bigger than that. He had lost his faith soon after leaving the home and had become a certified, card-carrying agnostic. He was now returning not to the church, but to fresh faith that he hoped would be pure, unadulterated, and without dogma, rituals, sacraments, or men in the middle. He was hoping that this night was about the real thing and he didn't want to pollute it with trappings of any sort. Ben made up his mind right then to not worship in temples made by men as he had in the past. His church would be the vast sanctuary of the sea. It was a beginning -- to what, he wasn't completely sure. He felt like he'd been found – that someone had actually been looking for him. It was like somebody had noticed that he was lost and alone. And now he knew, who.

Ben's friends wanted to take him out to celebrate his 'spiritual birthday.' They said it was what they did for anyone who had 'received Christ.' This didn't resonate with Ben. He hadn't joined any club and wasn't looking for an initiation, or whatever. He wanted to go somewhere to ponder this night. So he declined the invite and asked Olivia for a ride home. Ben had come to the church seeking a date and ended up meeting with destiny. That night he made another decision. He would no longer be a child of the streets. He decided to move in with Dave and his family.

Olivia pulled the car into the driveway of what used to be Ben's relative's home.

"Looks like everyone's in bed." "Do you want to talk for a bit?"

Ben knew he should tell her that he no longer lived here but realized that it would open up things that he wasn't ready to reveal to anyone yet.

"No, there's too much going around my head. I just need to go to bed."

Ben got out of the car and walked over to her window.

"Thanks for the ride, I'll see you tomorrow."

He watched her guide the car out of the driveway and was about to head toward the restaurant, when the car's back up lights came on. Olivia pulled back into the driveway and rolled her win-dow down.

"Do you still want to go out with me?" she asked.

CHAPTER 21

P eople didn't know what to make of it. The believers and the skeptics viewed Ben's newly found faith with suspicion. It didn't help that Ben would not attend the lunch time Bible studies, nor attend church on Sundays. Some of the believers used this to say that Ben wasn't really in. The skeptics took that as proof that nothing had changed, but Ben's teachers noticed a huge difference in him. For one, he sat quietly during class without seeking to be the center of attention. For another, he was turning in his homework on time. When Ben scored the highest grade in a science test his teacher was sure Ben had cheated. When they looked at all the scores, Ben had out-scored everybody by 15 points. So there was no one he could have cheated off and since the students were only allowed a pencil when they came into the classroom for a test a cheat sheet would have been noticed, as would any writing on his hands. They were worried and very concerned that he might be going under cover and planning a huge disruption, or maybe that he was depressed.

As such, he was a topic of discussion in the staff lunchroom and the students talked about him in the halls. Ben was oblivious to all this and stayed committed to his decision to not allow anything to pervert his newfound faith. He didn't feel a need to explain anything to anybody, or defend the decisions he had made. Ben was perfectly happy attending the church of the emerald wave. That was until he walked into science class the following day. The room was alive with the usual buzz and excitement as students found their seats. Dennis walked over and sat down next Ben.

"Dude, missed you at church."

"Church?"   "Bro, I was at Our Lady of the Emerald Wave. I never miss a Sunday. You should come visit sometime. Everybody's welcome."

They were about to get into the ongoing debate when Mr. Walters, Ben's favorite teacher called the room to order and began the science lesson.

"What is the estimated age of the earth?" He inquired.

Several hands shot up. Steve Hawkins yelled out. "4.54 fricken billion years old! I mean, 4.54 fricken billion years old, sir."

Walters continued with his questioning.

"What is that age based on . . . in detail, please?"

Total silence ensued followed by the students immediately going into various stages of trying to look busy to avoid being called on.

The teacher walked up and down the rows of students waiting for an answer. When no one could come up with one, Mr. Walters walked over to the blackboard and began to review the lesson talking about rocks, fossils, geologic time, and then into the eras, periods, and epochs, when in the back of the room a hand went up.

"Excuse me." A quiet voice asked.

Walters turned away from the blackboard. "Olivia?"

The Goth queen put her hand down. "What do you think of the Biblical account of creation? You know, the six day thing?"

Steve the jokester, shot out of his chair. "Get real! Why are you even asking?" You're gonna get the kooks in the class preaching at us again!"

That's all it took to turn the room into chaos filled with a mixture of scorn and laughter erupting all over.

One thing about Walters was that he never lost his cool. He simply motioned for the class to chill, and they did.

"Sit down, Mr. Hawkins. Olivia is asking a fair question. How many of you in the class accept the biblical account of creation, or as Olivia put it, the six day, thing?"

To everyone's amazement, Olivia's hand went up first, followed by a small number of the other students.

"Any of you care to defend your stance?" Walters asked as he sat down at his desk and waited.

"It's personal. I just believe it. I don't see a need to defend it," declared Olivia.

The teacher continued sitting in his chair and looked around the room. "Anybody else?"

When no one else responded the teacher walked back to the blackboard and began to write. Then in an uncustomary move Walters stopped writing and turned to readdress the class.

"While I have great respect for all faiths, as well as one's right to their own beliefs, my problem with the biblical account is with the reliability of the source, the Bible. It is filled with inconsistencies and contradictions."

With that statement, Mr. Walters continued to lecture as he diagramed the earth's timeline. Ben sat visibly stunned. He began to shift uncomfortably in his chair. He reached into his backpack for his Bible, and walked up to the teacher, and held his Bible out. "Show me one."

The room instantly became quiet . . . so quiet. Walters' eyes went from Ben to his Bible to the class and then back to Ben. After an eternity of seconds, the standoff ended.

"Please return to your seat, Mr. Storm." Walters was about to speak further when the bell rang. Once outside the room Ben was engulfed by the faithful.

Dennis pounded him on the back. "Dude! That was awesome!"

The hallway echoed with other statements of celebration over the pagans and unbelievers. Ben looked around with a quizzical look on his face.

"Hey!" "I was serious. I wasn't basing on Walters. I really need to know if the book is legit. If Walters knows something, I want to know. I wasn't crusading."

The hallway grew quiet as Ben walked away.

At the restaurant, Ben and the crew were putting stuff away and wiping down the counters. When they had finished, Dave walked over to the room where the time clock was located and punched out.

"Catch you guys later," Dave said as he left the kitchen. "Ben, see you this weekend right?" "Mom's been asking about you."

"Yeah, tell your folks I'll be there, Ben said as he walked into the dining room.

Lilly was busy rolling up silverware into napkins for the next day. Ben watched and wondered why he had never thought to ask her out. They had known each other since eighth grade and had hung out with the same circle of friends. She was beautiful and awesome and had this amazing sense of peace about her.

"Hey, can you bring me some more napkins, please?" Lilly yelled from the dining room.

Ben grabbed a pile of fresh napkins and joined her at the table.

"I heard about the big show down in Walters' class. Seems like you're the hero of the underdogs," Lilly teased.

"That's crap. You know Walters is my favorite teacher. The man is epic. He just shocked me by popping off about the Bible. I trust him and for him to be ripping on the Book, got to me. I wanted him to back up what he said to the class."

"What if he'd been right? What if he had been able to show you one? Lilly inquired. "I mean many people think the same thing about the Bible."

Lilly picked up the rolled dinner sets and headed off to the kitchen. "You have to settle that question of the Bible being legit for yourself. People are always going to try to discredit the Bible, misuse it to support agendas, and to cast shame and fear. You have to decide who you're going to believe, and you have to get into the Book so you know what's in it."

Ben sat reflecting on the question. He hadn't expected such sudden challenges to his newfound faith -- especially not from his favorite teacher. Finally, Ben said, "I'm sleeping. I haven't slept for more than five hours for the past year. Now I sleep so sound, and I'm dreaming. My heart has stopped pounding and I no longer hear my pulse in my right ear. The wildest thing though is that I have this crazy renewed sense of hope." He wanted to tell her that none of these made sense because he was still homeless living by his street smarts, and day to day. All he knew at the moment was that God was near and He was speaking to him out of a Book, and that was all.

"What if Walters is right? What if next week he's able to show you contradictions in the Bible? What would you do?"

"I guess I'd go back to my, just me and the universe, karma, fate, or whatever, ways." He replied. "If it's not legit, it's just another holy book. I need more than that."

Lilly and Ben stood outside the restaurant for a few more minutes talking softly. "Do you want a ride to your uncle's?" She offered.

"No, I'm good. You've given me a lot to think about, I'll walk." Ben waited until Lilly left then he turned and walked to the back door of the restaurant and unlocked the door. That night he dreamt of bearded wise men spouting theology, hordes of angry people rushing a church, and that Lilly was his sister. Crazy.

Ben's decision did have ramifications, mostly social. Some of his former friends stopped coming around saying he wasn't fun anymore. Others didn't get the Jesus freak thing. He no longer hung around Kenny, and some of the girls. This didn't make sense to Ben. If Kenny and the others had decided to become Buddhist, Hari Krishna, or children of the universe, whatever -- he was good with that. Why talk smack about him because of his choice?

Surprisingly, Walters made it a point to find Ben and follow through on the classroom incident. He found Ben in the locker room getting ready for practice. The coach wasn't sure how to approach the topic. He felt bad for his comments, and disappointed in himself for speaking in such a biased manner. Coach Walters had always been careful in sharing personal information and beliefs. Why he had reacted to Olivia's question resulted in some deep reflection. He had always considered himself fair and open-minded. The last thing he wanted to do was to squash young faith no matter how much he disagreed. The coach walked over to Ben and sat on the bench.

"Ben, I'm sorry for my comments concerning the Bible. It was wrong of me. I'll apologize to the rest of the class next time we meet."

The coach stuck out his hand. Ben had never heard an adult apologize. Never. It was an unsettling moment. The man he most respected in his life was saying he was sorry. The coach was about to withdraw his hand, when Ben reached out to shake it.

"Thanks, coach." That's all he could think of to say.

"Then, we're OK?" asked the coach.

Ben stood up, "We're fine."

CHAPTER 22

D ave's room had been rearranged so that Ben could have some space. Their late night philosophical talks became a nightly event. They would talk into the early morning hours, even on school nights. Ben loved falling asleep to the radio, a luxury he had never enjoyed while living in the orchard or at the restaurant for fear of being discovered. For whatever reason though, Ben kept his bags packed even though Dave had given him a couple of his drawers for his belongings. His experience had taught him that everything is temporary. Nevertheless, he was enjoying living at Dave's and he decided to ride this wave until there wasn't one.

Moving into Dave's also brought him closer to the Bible study lunch group, which he attended sporadically out of a desire to know more about the Book. He had been reading the Bible every day and had accumulated a ton of questions, especially after reading through Genesis and on to Leviticus. There were some weird happenings going on. If it had been him writing the story, he'd have left some of the characters out.

What he liked most about the group was the activities and events like the concert they decided to put together after meeting a group of longhairs that played acid rock for Jesus.

The seniors were hanging out in the Quad swapping stories of summer when Ben was called to the school office over the intercom. When he arrived at Mr. Barlow's office, he noticed a pile of flyers sitting on his desk like the ones they had just pasted all over the school to announce the concert.

"Did you get these posters approved?" Barlow asked

Ben innocently replied. "By who?"

Mr. Barlow stood up and walked around his desk to where Ben stood. "By me! Where did you get these?"

Ben thought for a moment and then decided to tell it like it was. "I know this is gonna sound whacked, but uh, God gave them to us to let people know about our concert."

Barlow's veins bulged in his neck. His face turned nuclear reactor disaster code red as he bellowed, "Listen here, funny boy, you have thirty minutes to take those flyers down, all of them!"

Ben walked out of the office like a chastised prophet to give his friends the news. "Let's go," he said, "we gotta take the flyers down."

Dave immediately took issue with the demand. "Why? Who sez?"

"Barlow. He's pissed. Seems we should have asked to put them up. Can't put up religious stuff on campus. News to me, but that's how it is, we better get going," Ben advised.

"Wait. What about religious freedom and freedom of expression and stuff?" Olivia demanded. "Besides our concert is not a religious event, it's a concert."

Ben just wanted to get on with it. He wasn't looking for a fight with Barlow. "Hey, it's no big. Let's just do it."

"Stop," she called after him, "we asked God for those flyers remember? We didn't have the cash, and God provided. He gave them to us to put up."

Without looking back at her, Ben responded, "I told Barlow that."

"You told Barlow God gave them to us?" Dennis asked more amused than inquiring.

"Yeah, he asked me where we had gotten them." Ben replied.

Dennis spoke with the group. "Fair enough. Let's take them down. He's been warned. Barlow is dealing with God, not us."

Olivia shook her head. "Dude, do you always have to be such a zealot? Ben and I will put them up so that we don't all get nailed."

Later just as the school day was ending, Ben again heard himself being called to Mr. Barlow's office. The man sat calmly at his desk as Ben entered.

"Mr. Storm, didn't I tell you to remove all your flyers from school property?"

"Yes, sir, and we did." Ben replied respectfully.

Mr. Barlow walked to his window. "Then why is this school still plastered with your posters? Did God put them back up?"

Ben answered knowing he was in deep kimchi. "No sir, Olivia and I did. No disrespect intended but like I told you, God gave them to us. We did what you asked, we took them down, but I think He intended for students to see them. We'll take them down after school."

After school Olivia and Ben were sent directly to detention where they sat with the students from the wild side of their high school. Tough guys and girls who made hairy eyeballs at them as they walked into the room and started giving them a hard time.

A colossal guy got in Ben's face and mocked him. "What are you in here for peaches, slurping your milk too loud?" His girl friend joined in as she sneered at Olivia, "Probably a lover's quarrel right in the middle of class! How horrid!"

Ben and Olivia found a place to sit and ignored the kooks. They took out work they had brought and settled in for the next 55 minutes.

That weekend the concert was packed with students. The long hairs cranked out acid-rock music for Jesus, just like they said they would. At the end of the night the band passed out Bibles for free and stayed and talked with the students until the janitor came and kicked everybody out.

CHAPTER 23

The drawers in Dave's room reserved for Ben's stuff were still empty even though Ben had been living there for three months. As Christmas came, the house took on a look that Ben had not seen since he had left St. Margaret's. It had been a long time since he had sat next to a Christmas tree and he never tired of seeing the festive decorations and bright lights when he arrived at Dave's house after work.

One weekend as Ben walked through the Mall, he stopped to listen to a youth brass band doing Christmas Jazz. He was so completely wrapped up in the music that he failed to notice Lilly standing next to him.

"Hmmm. seems the Grinch has been redeemed! I thought you didn't do Christmas," she teased.

Ben dropped his shopping list and looked up startled. "Dang Lil, you scared me."

They walked over to a bench and sat down. "Dave's folks make a big deal of it."

"Back at the home Christmas was the highlight of the year. I guess it's just been on the back burner for me. Who knows though? Even you might benefit from my change of heart and receive a gift."

On Christmas Eve, Ben told Dave that he had decided to attend Midnight Mass at the Catholic Church nearby. He walked into the packed auditorium and sat scanning the icons of the Saints, and stained glass. The music and the incense floated in the air, followed by the chanting of the Christmas story from the Gospel of Luke. Ben was instantly transported to a distant place and to days gone by. He had every part of the service memorized from his many years as an altar boy. When the service was over, he waited until the people had left and walked to the front of church, where he lit a candle before the Christ child.

Looking around Dave's living room, Ben smiled. The room was trashed with gift-wrappings and boxes. Dave's family and Ben were soaking in the joy of the season when the phone rang. Mrs. Menner got up to answer it, and came back in the room with the phone. "It's for you, Ben"

He took the phone and walked into the other room. "Hello?"

"You goofball!" laughed Lilly on the other end. "You didn't have to get me a gift!"

A huge smile broke out on Ben's face. "You found it!" "I put it in your apron at work on Friday. When you didn't say anything I thought I'd put it in the wrong apron."

"You did, koo-koo head!" Lilly replied. Lee gave it to me. It was in his wife's apron. She thought it was for her and was so happy with Lee until she saw my name on the package. You almost got him in trouble, silly!"

"Well, do you like it?" Ben asked.

"I do, it's awesome. Thanks, Ben. Hope your Christmas is going great at Dave's, see you at work,"

The other adventures that Ben had enjoyed, was the winter camp that happened two months later. He had resisted at first, but gave in once he heard about the hot girls that went to winter camp. That February, Dave, Ben, Lilly, and some friends stopped at a vending machine to buy snacks before the evening chapel program. Ben pulled the lever and a bag of jellybeans slid down. He shoved the packet into his jeans pocket and walked on with the group.

There were hundreds of teens standing up getting into the music as a band played on a stage lit up to look like a concert venue. Fog floated along the base of the stage and up toward the ceiling. Ben and his friends slid into the last available bench.

"This happen every year?" Ben asked as he scanned the room.

Lilly shrugged her shoulders. "Yep. It gets trendier every time though. "Fog? Seriously?"

They watched as a 20-something guy with faded jeans, a t-shirt covered by outer shirt with sleeves rolled up to show his tattoos walked on stage. He began ranting about the dangers of current teen culture. Ben was busy trying to get a grip on what the guy was so mad about when one of the camp counselors stood next to where Ben was sitting.

"Is this seat taken?" she asked with a kind smile.

Ben gave her a standoffish look and reluctantly scooted over. He returned his attention to the speaker who was ranting on, warning teens about the many things in the world that would pull them away from God. Eventually, Ben got bored and reached into his jeans for his snack, only to have the noise of the cellophane package get the woman's attention. She looked down to see what the noise was.

All he could think of to say was, "Do you want a jelly bean?"

The lady broke out in a big smile and replied, "I love jelly beans! Sure, my name is Joyce."

"Ah, I'm Ben."

At the end of the night, the teens streamed out into the night. Ben and his friends were walking back to their cabins when Joyce walked by.

"Thanks for the jelly beans, Ben." Joyce called to him.

The guys gave Ben puzzled looks. Only Gary had the nerve to ask what they were all thinking. "Dude, were you sharing jelly beans with that lady?"

Dave laughed out. "Well, we did come here to pick up chicks, right? It's his new girlfriend! Ben's always gone after the older ones."

"Hey, she caught me sneaking jelly beans. She could have done the . . . 'no food in the chapel thing.' So, yeah, I gave her some. So what?"

"Touchy!" "See? Told you," Dave mocked. "He digs her."

The next day Ben was sitting by himself journaling. Joyce saw him and walked over. "Hey, Ben."

He looked around to make sure none of the guys were close by. "Hey."

"What church did you come with?" She asked.

"I came with Bethel. Jack and Darlene Hoffa are my pastors," he volunteered.

Joyce's eyes lit up. "I know Jack and Darlene! Wonderful people."

She soon picked up Ben's uncomfortable vibe. Joyce handed Ben a bag of jellybeans and started to walk away, then stopped.

"I know we just met, and that all I know about you Ben, is that you love jelly beans, and that we have some mutual friends, but I wanted you to know that I'm praying for you."

Ben didn't know what to do with that information or even how to respond. He mumbled something and walked away.

At dinner, the campers' chatter echoed off the metal roof of the dining hall. Ben and his friends ditched the girls from Bethel to scam on the girls from First Prez. Dennis led them to a table nearby. "H-e-l-l-o, ladies. May I and my fine friends join you?"

Ben noticed Joyce sitting by herself and walked over to join her. They guys watched him walk away.

"Told you, he's got it bad for that woman," said Frank

"Hey, Joyce." Ben placed his tray down on the table.

"Ben!" She looked up pleasantly surprised.

Joyce began to make small talk. He didn't mean to be rude, but Ben had a purpose in meeting with her, so he cut her off. "Why are you praying for me? Every time I see you, you tell me, you're praying for me. I feel like I'm being spiritually stalked."

Ben felt immediately remorseful. "I'm sorry. I didn't mean it to come off like that."

Joyce didn't seem offended. "I don't know why I'm praying for you. I just feel like God wants to do something very special for you this week."

"Hmm, something special, he mused in his head as he picked at his food. What would that be?" Ben looked up at Joyce. "I don't know what that means, but I hope it's good." He stood up to leave. "Thanks, I guess, for praying for me. It's still a bit new to me, but thanks."

When camp ended, teens were boarding various buses for departure. Camp romances were sadly ending -- others were parting with promises to keep the heart flames burning. Joyce walked over to Ben and handed him a box. "Open this on the bus. I am so glad I met you, Ben."

The bus turned onto the highway. Ben looked out of the window, and then reached for Joyce's gift. As he opened the box, a note fell out. He leaned down to pick the note off the floor and read it.

"Ben, the God I know doesn't toy with us, and He will never waste our pain. Somehow, pain will always have a purpose, like some sort of preparation thing, maybe. Anyway, I hope you like the necklace, the dove represents the Holy Spirit, who Jesus gave us as our Helper -- the olive branch is for peace. I wish you tons of peace."

CHAPTER 24

The spring monsoons began to fall as spring arrived and with it came the last hurrah of the flu. Ben was laid up in bed sick to his stomach and with a terrible pounding in his head. All of sudden he heard the door slam and then the loud yelling of Dave's mom.

"You need to leave. Now! Get out! Did you really think I wouldn't find them? Take your beloved bottles and get out!"

Ben bolted up in his bed. Was he hallucinating? Was she talking to him? What was going on? He heard Dave's dad yell back in his own defense, then slammed the bedroom door. Mrs. Menner banged on the door.

"Come out of there, damn you!" She demanded.

When he refused to come out she ran through the house grabbing all the bottles she had found and began throwing them out the front door where they smashed into pieces, raining booze all over the driveway and the front yard. She saw her husband's car backing out of the garage and ran to it pounding on the window.

"You liar! You promised, you promised." She wailed.

It got really quiet. Ben didn't know what to do. Maybe it would be better if she didn't know that he had heard everything. He waited and when he heard quiet sobbing coming from downstairs, he decided to check on her.

"Beth, are you all right?" he gently asked.

"You heard all that, didn't you?" she sadly asked.

"Yeah." Ben admitted.

Dave came flying in the house. "Mom? Mom! Dad said I needed to get home quick. What happened?"

Dave's mom called to him from where she and Ben sat. "In here, Dave."

Her son's concern turned into embarrassment when he saw Ben sitting with his mom. "Uh, Ben, could you give us some space?"

"Sure, I'll be outside." Ben responded.

Dave hugged his heart-broken mother as she began to tell him an old story.

"What always happens is he promises me he's done with the bottle and I find one, then two. He hasn't been at work for a week. Marv called me and asked if he was sick. It's how I found out. When I was restocking my supplies in my office I discovered his stash. I told him to go. I'm certain Ben heard and saw it all."

Dave sat down dejected. "Dad seemed to be doing so good. Like he was really trying. I guess I have some explaining to do to Ben. Will dad be coming back?"

"No. I'm filing for divorce. I'm sorry, Dave, he won't change. He's had 25 years. We'll have to sell the house. Ben can still live with us wherever we go. I'm truly sorry," she said.

Dave went outside and found Ben sitting on the fence looking out at the empty field behind their house.

"Hey Ben. Sorry about all the drama. I don't really know what to say."

"It's not your fault. I know this scene. I lived with my dad for one year. He was the same way. I had never met him before and was so happy to have my own home with a dad. Didn't last long. He loved the bottle too. I sort of had an idea your dad was partaking."

"How did you know? Dave asked.

"I came home a couple of times and saw him passed out on the couch." Ben continued. "First time I thought he was dead. I went over and pounded on his chest and he let out this massive exhale. It scared the hell out of me. I got a whiff of that old familiar smell. I knew."

Oh my God, Ben, "Why didn't you tell us?

"I didn't think it was my place. I'm sorry. I should have," Ben replied with regret.

"Don't have to be sorry. I should have seen it coming. Guess I was just hoping he would really give it up this time. My mom is going to file for divorce. She's selling the house which means we'll be moving, but you can still live with us" Dave offered.

"Thanks. I'm taking a walk so you and your mom have a chance to talk more. When I come back, I'll help with the mess in the driveway." Ben hopped the fence and stepped out into the field.

Visibly upset and confused, Ben followed a well-trodden cow trail. He'd been walking for some time ruminating about the twists that kept occurring in his life. Just when things seemed to be settling down, it'd go haywire again. He wasn't sure what to do, should he go back to the restaurant?

In the distance, Ben noticed a grove of trees. He felt strongly drawn to them as if he were magnetized. When he arrived at the grove he sat on a log, and sensed something powerful and mysterious. Everything around him was still and incredibly quiet. Ben felt a prompting to look around. He studied the trees, then chose one of them and climbed it. He was startled to see sitting on one of the massive branches, a huge owl looking at him from its perch. Ben froze and waited to see what the owl would do, but it just sat look-ing at him with as much curiosity in him as Ben had about the owl. It was like they were having a staring contest. Ultimately, the owl won. Who can out stare an owl? Ben carefully backed away from the branch and hopped down to the ground. The owl followed his every move. He turned to look back at the tree as he walked away. "I'll be back," he said to the owl.

When he returned to the house, Ben joined Dave in the front yard and helped him clean up the mess.

"Where'd you go?" Dave asked.

" I guess you can call it cattle trail therapy. I went walking following the cow trails, thinking and stuff."

Dave waited for Ben to say more. Finally he said, "What did you come up with?'

"I don't know, but I won't be living with you guys. You and your mom need time to settle in." Ben answered. "I'll be all right. On a brighter note, I can't wait for the fireside at the beach tonight. We both need it."

The guys pulled into the beach parking lot and joined their friends who were sitting around a fire ring. Dave began jamming on the guitar, as Lilly, Olivia, and others arrived. Lilly pulled Ben away from the fire. "Dave told me you're moving out."

"Yeah, that's right," he confirmed.

"Where to? You're not going back to your uncle's -- how about our place?"

"With Jeanie and Howie gone, it's just me and my folks. We've got plenty of room. My mom and dad are solid. It'll be a good home for you at least until we graduate."

"Lil thanks, but I'm OK. Really," he reassured her. "Come on let's get back to the group." He was trying to decide if he should mention the tree thing, fearing that she would think he was a toon.

They were still a ways from the fireside when he cautiously said, "Lil, something really weird happened to me today. Scary almost. Do you believe you can feel God?"

Lilly stopped walking, "What do you mean?"

"After I found out that Dave's folks were calling it quits and that we'd have to move, I went walking in the field behind Dave's house. I ended up in some grove. It was like I was drawn there. I was sitting on a log letting God have it for my crappy life when all of a sudden it got really quiet and still -- seriously, no sound. I felt like this massive peace come over me and like if I had put my arm out, it would have landed on a shoulder," Ben offered.

The two sat in silence. It seemed to take forever for Lil to answer.

"Why are you thinking it was God?"

Ben sighed with relief. Lilly was taking this serious. "I don't know, but of all the times I've shot prayers out to Him, this time, the time I'm fully ragging on Him, I felt like He really heard me and that it's all going to work out. I'll find a place that'll be what I need and that won't blow up in my face again."

"I've never had an experience like that. I don't know what to tell you except that my offer still stands. My folks will let you stay with us, " Lilly responded.

That night sitting around the fire ring with his friends, Ben watched the embers rise up into the night sky and evaporate. There was a full moon in the sky and down at the shore the grunion were running. They came in with each wave, did their business and retreated back to the ocean with the next wave. It was all part of a process, the huge process of all life and like the grunion -- he too, was attempting to make use of the waves -- the tumultuous waves of the unknown.

CHAPTER 25

G oing back to school after Spring Break is like going in for a root canal. Nobody looks forward to it, not even the teachers, and certainly not the janitors. Ben kept looking at the clock in his classrooms and was sure they were all running late. The day was dragging and driving him crazy. It took all the discipline he had to not get up and leave during his last period class. When the last bell rang, Ben jetted out of the room and took off running to Dave's house where he had hid a lounge chair mattress and some supplies in his backyard, covered by a tarp. He knew it would be safe there because the family had moved out and the house was empty and being shown to prospective buyers. Ben grabbed everything, hopped the fence, and began the long walk to the grove, dragging the mattress behind him.

When he arrived, Ben walked around the tree looking up among the branches for the owl. He didn't realize the owl was already looking at him and following his every move. When Ben did spot him, he tossed a meat scrap to the owl.

"Here you go. First month's rent," he offered.

Walking among the oaks Ben noticed that the ones closest to the field were in rows like they had been intentionally planted. The oaks behind however were scattered, or stood in groups of three or four. He also took note of the silence. The silence that at first unnerved him, but later would serve to calm him. A silence that was broken only when the oaks allowed it to be, giving the wind, the birds, the bugs, and other creatures of the field permission to speak or sing.

The tree Ben chose was massive. It had the scars of battles with lightening, drought, and bores. The oak had stood its ground for a hundred years never wavering, never bowing to adversity. Its canopy spread wide infiltrating the canopy of its neighbor, and whose canopy in turn spread into the oak next to him. The gnarled truck rose eight feet from the ground before sending branches high and wide.

His English class had just finished reading John Steinbeck's, Cannery Row. Ben remembered seeing illustrations of the fish canning shops talked about in the book. Shacks in rows bustled with the actions of fishmongers along the piers in Monterey. He looked out at the rows of oaks with their thick canopies and stout branches and proclaimed that his place of abode would now and forever more be known as Canopy Row.

He got busy setting up house. The canopy of the tree was so dense that it acted as a roof. Since there was a constant rain of acorns and leaves, Ben took the green tarp and tied it to the branches overhead to protect him from the downpour. On the nights that the wind did not blow causing the acorns to fall, he would roll the tarp up so that he could see the points of lights entering through the thick leaves. He found a place among the branches that formed a natural cradle and would prevent him from rolling off in his sleep, and placed the mattress there. Ben also found several broken branches where he could hang a battery-powered lantern and the bags that held his clothes and his books. He decided to place his food in the tree nearby to avoid attracting animals to his tree and give him time to prepare if one did show up. Finally, Ben attached the rope and wooden ladder he had made to a thick branch. He had designed it so that he could release it while he was on the ground so that he could climb the tree, and so that he could pull the ladder up once he was in the tree. His pad was ready. He was home.

At night Ben lay on the lounge mattress wrapped up in his sleeping bag safe among the foliage of the oak. The music of the fields was lulling him to sleep but not before he saw the owl leave for her nightly meal.

"This is going to work," he thought. "I come home to sleep and the owl goes out to hunt. The owl comes home to sleep and I go off to school. We're going to be the perfect roommates."

Living in the oak tree was like being back at the orange orchard -- only better. He was a good distance from any house and the closest road was at least two miles away. Ben walked that distance every night, most of it in pitch darkness after he had gotten off work. It never bothered him. He was excelling at school, the gymnastic team he was on was going to CIF State Championships, and he had all the money and food he needed. It would be difficult to find a more contented or grateful dude anywhere. He was talking with God on a regular basis, but had yet to feel relaxed in His presence. He had no idea what he would do if he ever did hear a response. He wondered if the voice that first gave him the plan, had been God. Was it He that had been guiding him along all the time even while Ben was actively rejecting Him? As it was, it still freaked him out the times when the presence was so strong in the grove.

As Ben approached the restaurant the next day, the sky opened up and let loose a torrent of rain. Waiting at a stoplight, he watched the raindrops splatter on the windshield only to have their fragments whisked aside by the wiper.

"Guess I won't be sleeping at home tonight," he realized.

He decided to initiate his back up plan and snuggle up in the restaurant booth to sleep. He was glad that he thought to hide a blanket and a small pillow in the pantry. All he could think of as he lay in the booth that night was the effect of the rain on his pad and how the owl was faring. A humorous thought flashed through his mind of the owl sitting on his mattress under the green tarp snug as a bug. It would be just like her.

Fortunately, Ben was off the following day, so after school he made a dash for home.

The owl sat on her branch and with big yellow eyes watched as Ben spread out his sleeping bag and clothes in the grass to dry. She screeched at him when he got a bit too close climbing the tree.

"Whoa there. Sorry to wake you, I'll be quiet."

CHAPTER 26

On the weekend, the Graziano crews were prepping food for the evening crowd. Ben was in and out of the restaurant all night making the time fly by. He kept trying to find some time to call Olivia, but he never got the chance. Every time he returned from making a delivery another one was waiting for him. He was relieved when it was time to switch jobs for the night with Dave so he could stay and help make pizzas instead. Still due to the packed house he never got around to calling her. It would have to wait.

When the closed sign was hung the crew all jumped in to clear the tables, wash the dishes and get things ready for the next day. It was past midnight when they walked out the door.

"Come on Ben, let's get a donut and I'll give you a ride home," offered Dave.

That piqued everyone's interest because Ben's friends had been wondering where he had moved.

"No, not tonight," Ben answered. "I'm beat."

"Then I'll just give you a ride home." Dave insisted.

Ben tried to politely refuse a ride but when his friends kept pressuring him to give in, he walked off. "I told you I don't need a ride."

Ben walked away without hearing someone suggest they follow him, but Lilly shut that down. She figured if he wanted them to know where he lived, he'd tell them. Although she wanted to be reassured that Ben was really OK, she told the guys to get in their cars and leave Ben alone.

Before Ben clocked in at work the next day, he walked to a phone booth and dialed.

"Olivia? Hey, it's Ben." He had planned to go into a bit of small talk, but in the heat of the moment, he choked and just blurted out, "Do you have a date for the prom?" He asked as he fidgeted with the door handle in the phone booth.

"Ben, when have I ever gone to a dance at Rowland?"

Ben shifted from foot to foot and wiped his sweating hands on his pant leg. "Would you go with me?"

"You're asking me out?" she asked hesitantly.

"Yeah, I am," Ben confirmed.

"OK, ah, sure," Olivia accepted.

Ben couldn't think of anything else to say. So he decided to call it good and hang up. "Great, let me know what color your dress will be," he added.

Olivia candidly replied, "Ben, I'm Goth. What do you think?"

After hanging up with Ben, She sat on her bed with the phone still in her hand and looked at herself in the mirror. "I'm going with a surfer to the prom. Me! The Goth queen going with Kahuna -- to a prom!"

Laying in his sleeping bag, Ben rehearsed everything he had to do to get ready for the dance. Dave had agreed to let him get ready at his house. They would go and get tuxes before work that weekend, and somehow he found black roses for Olivia's corsage. He surprised himself at how excited he was about the date. Ben had also thought to have Olivia pick him up at Dave's. He felt a bit lame about having her pick him up but she had insisted saying she had a surprise for him. Lilly came up to him at lunch and teased, "Hey Romeo, I heard you've broken your, 'you'll never catch me at a dance,' vow. Who's your date?"

"You'll see." That's all Ben had to say about that.

A vintage 57 T-Bird pulled up to Dave's driveway and honked for Ben. He came out of the house looking very GQ, but with the goofiest look on his face as he marveled at the incredible car and the glamorous driver in the front seat. When they arrived at the hotel, Olivia smoothly brought the car to the curb and let Ben out. She peeled out and went to park the car. The guys were standing with gaping mouths as a stunning Olivia returned to join Ben. She was wearing a long black silk oriental themed dress with silver pearl brocade over one of her shoulders. To say that it was form fitting would be an understatement. The girl was doing justice to the dress. She had worn her hair down with loose curls cascading to her shoulders. Her make-up was perfect.

"Gentlemen, I think you know Olivia. We were all in science together," Ben remarked casually.

The ballroom was packed wall to wall with bodies. Ben and Olivia stood along the wall feeling awkward and out of place. Feelings of guilt hammered on Ben's conscience for bring her to the event. "Bad idea huh? Wanna go?"

She looked around, "Let's dance one song, then go."

Lucky for Ben the next song the band played was a slow one. It was one of those long, slow songs that all guys pray will play when they finally get to dance with 'that' girl. When the song ended, Ben and Olivia continued to hold on to each other. Dave walked over and tapped Ben on the shoulder. "Dude, song's over."

That dance led to another, and then more. They ended up dominating the dance floor. During the last dance, as he was swaying to the music, Ben realized what a fortunate man he was. He was dancing with the babe of the ball. He opened his eyes and clung close to Olivia just to make sure it was really all happening.

After the prom, the couple jetted out of the room and ran to the car. Olivia backed the car out of the parking spot. "Where to?"

Ben had been planning this night for weeks. "Let's go to where I work. I make a great pizza. It'll just be us."

He unlocked the door, and led her to the kitchen.

Everything was laid out on the counter. He went into the walk-in fridge and came back with two small mounds of pizza dough. "Here, rub some flour in your hands, then start kneading the dough from the inside and go out.

Olivia followed Ben's motions. "Like this?"

"That's it! You're a natural. Keep doing that until it's the size of a plate."

When she had stretched out her dough, Ben showed her how to flip it in the air to increase the size. After several failed attempts Olivia was soon spinning pizza in the air while flour fell like snow all around them.

After the pizzas were placed in the oven, Ben led her to a booth in the dining room. The table was set with fine China, silverware, crystal goblets, and candles. He brought over a chilled bottle of their favorite drink -- Mug Root Beer, and deftly poured her a drink. Ben went into the kitchen and returned with an antipasto salad, and some breadsticks, then slid in across from her. He lifted up his glass.

"To this night," he toasted.

"To this night," Olivia agreed.

He walked over to the jukebox and selected "Something" by The Beatles, then walked back to the booth and extended his hand.

That's how the night ended, dancing to love songs. When dawn came, they climbed into the T-bird and drove through a Jack in the Box for breakfast which they ate sitting on the pier watching the first rays of the sun reflecting off the water and individually hoping that love would stay.

CHAPTER 27

After youth group, Gary and the guys were waiting for Ben to finish talking with Olivia so they could leave. Tom shouted out, "Let's go! Kiss her and say good night already!"

Ben sauntered to the car, "You cave-dwellers have no sense of romance," taunted Ben. "Can you drop me off by Dave's old house. I live close by."

Gary called out from the back seat, "Who are you living with now?"

"A cousin of mine. We're sharing a condo. It's a good set up."

Jack pulled over. The guys watched Ben walk to a condo complex and drove off.

"Does that sound sketchy to anybody else?" Gary asked suspiciously.

"Yup. The dude totally is misleading us. Turn around, let's follow him."

Gary switched off the engine and car lights, they watched as Ben hopped a fence and disappeared into the darkness. They waited for a few minutes then quietly stepped out of the car to follow Ben into the pitch-black field.

"Turn the flashlight on!" commanded Tom.

"Quiet, dork! No lights."

Ben froze. He realized he was being followed. He stepped off the path and hid behind a bush and watched the guys walk by warily. Ben waited until they had gone a few yards. He let out a blood-curdling scream and then gave chase, yelling as he ran after the guys.

Gary yelled, Tom took off running, Jack dropped to the ground. Ben calmly walked up.

"What are you guys doing?" He asked.

"Crap! What the heck, Ben?" Gary fumed.

Tom came back from running off. Jack peeled himself off the ground. Gary remained torqued.

"You guys following me?" Ben asked matter of fact like.

"Yeah, we are, so what?" "Let's see your condo," Jack replied.

Ben decided to play along with the guys. "All right, let's go."

The group set out for Ben's tree fully expecting Ben to tell them he was just messing with them, but he continued to calmly lead the way. After walking awhile the guys were getting spooked.

"Good thing you guys are wearing your jackets. It gets a bit chilly out here at night," Ben commented.

Tom hesitantly offered a suggestion. "Let's stop here. You can show us where you live in the morning." The rest of the guys chimed in with agreement.

"Are you sure?" The ground is wet and will get wetter by morning," cautioned Ben.

Gary was quick to offer up a solution. "Hey, I have a couple of sleeping bags in my car and some blankets."

"Better yet, why don't we just come back in the daylight?" Tom suggested.

Ben waited to see what they would decide. He was hoping for Tom's option then he could say he was just kidding, but he knew the guys would not let him off the hook. They would demand to see where he was living.

"Why don't you guys go get Gary's bags and stuff -- I'll wait here," he instructed.

Everyone had just settled in on the bags talking, when a wild chorus surrounded the guys.

"Damn." Ben sighed.

"What was that?" pleaded Tom.

"Quiet!" "Don't move," Ben instructed. "It's the band of rogue coyotes. They've been killing the calves in the pasture. We'll take turns doing watch. Gary, you take the first watch. When you're done wake up Tom. Jack, you'll go next, then wake me up."

"Ok, Ben. Should I get a stick or something?" Gary asked.

"Naw, just let us know if you see them and we'll play dead," Ben briefed him.

Jack spat out, "seriously, that's our plan -- we play dead?" "I say we run."

"You do, and you'll be dinner," Ben warned.

Eventually the guys laid down and tried to sleep. Ben looked over at Gary who was intently peering into the night. An hour later Ben heard Gary wake up Tom.

Tom sat up from a deep sleep and instantly was alert. No rouge coyote was having him for dinner. "OK. Gary thanks."

He stood his watch with great seriousness. Tom was a bundle of nerves by the time his shift was over. Every noise had caused him concern. He gratefully reached over to wake up Jack and passed out. After Jack had completed his watch he woke up Ben who waited until Jack lay back down and then he went back to sleep. The coyote band that was causing so much anxiety among his friends, was but one of the sounds in the night that helped him drift off to sleep. As dawn came, Ben woke up and reached over for Gary.

"Dude, wake up -- you're on," he commanded. By the time the rotation got back to Jack the sun was baking them in their sleep-ing bags. Jack stumbled out of from under his blanket. "You're messing with us right? You don't live out here."

Tom was not a happy camper. "Not funny Ben, -- crap, we could have been coyote Alpo!"

"Hey, you guys followed me. It was your idea, but yeah I really do live out here. You guys cannot tell anybody about this. Come on," Ben admitted.

They left their stuff on the hillside where they had spent the night and Ben led them to the grove and to his tree. The guys stood in awe and marvel at Ben's condo.

Gary spoke for everyone. "Boss!" he exclaimed.

In an instant everyone began to climb the tree.

"Keep it down. My roomie's sleeping" Ben requested.

The guys looked over to see an owl glaring at them.

"Ben, you're Robinson fricken Caruso!" "This is boss!" Jack blurted out.

When they had explored the tree and the surrounding area, they sat among the branches.

"OK. Promise me you won't tell anybody about this," Ben pleaded. "I'm stoked living here. I've got all the food I need, I'm making money and I'm doing great in school. I don't need a rescue. Got it?" "If you guys tell anybody, I could end up in a foster home. Our secret, OK?"

The guys agreed and made a pact that the secret would be kept. They spit in their palms and gave each other sincere and binding handshakes. The group spent the day exploring and climbing the various trees in the grove. As the day was ending, they made a plan to go and pick up some supplies, more sleeping bags and return to spend the night. All of them had told their parent's that they would be spending the night at Ben's, which was the truth. They spread their bags out at the base of the oak and fell quickly asleep.

Later that night Ben grabbed his flashlight and read out of Psalms -- "When I consider your heavens, the work of your fingers, the moon and the stars, which you have set in place, what is mankind that you are mindful of them, human beings that you care for them?"

He closed the book and flipped off the flashlight. The dark closed in on him and his friends, exposing the billions of stars above them, sending beams of light filtering through the oak's leaves.

CHAPTER 28

Most high school relationships are about as sustainable as hitting an F#4 note by a tone-deaf choir. There are exceptions, and so far, Ben and Olivia appeared to be strong contenders for going beyond two months. They had experienced their share of misunderstandings, unintentional slights, and stepped on several relational land mines. There had been plenty of give and take and both had made sacrifices for the sake of the relationship. Ben had even started attending Olivia's church just so he could spend more time with her.

Dave and Lilly were teasing Ben about him and Olivia getting voted most romantic couple when the phone rang.

Ben wiped his hands and grabbed the receiver. "Hello? Hey Olivia! Hi. Sure, yeah, my break is at five. Yeah, pick me up then."

The shift seemed to last forever. Ben tried to stop checking the clock. His break was only an hour away. He kept busy so that the time would pass quickly. At the same time he couldn't help but wonder what was on Olivia's mind. Ben was deep in thought when he heard a car horn. He took off his apron, dried off his hands, and headed toward the parking lot.

Olivia reached over to unlock the door.

"What a great surprise! What's up?" Ben asked."

The car pulled out of the driveway. She hadn't said a word.

Ben was confused which quickly turned to worry. "Olivia, what's wrong?"

She pulled the car over and began to weep. Ben felt helpless. He had no idea what was going on and her crying unnerved him. Finally, between her sobs she gave Ben the worst possible news. "I can't go out with you anymore."

"You're breaking up with me? Why?" Ben pleaded.

Olivia turned her face away from Ben. She was unable to look him in the eye.

"Yes, I'm sorry."

Ben's mind was short-circuiting. A million emotions were streaking like meteors through his brain. He was having a difficult time finding words to string together into sentences. Somehow he managed to say, "Just like that, we're over?"

She didn't respond. Olivia sat in her seat with her head down. Ben looked out the front window waiting. When an answer didn't come he got out of the car and began walking back to the restaurant.

It took Ben a while to get back to work. He walked in looking drained and stepped into the cooler. When he didn't come out, Lilly opened the door.

"Hey, you're an hour late from your lunch, Ben. Lee is not pleased."

Ben walked out, headed to the sink and began washing the tower of dishes that had accumulated in his absence. Lee was the least of his issues. Lilly walked over to the sink. "Are you gonna tell me what happened?"

"It doesn't matter. I'm all right," he sighed.

On the walk back to the tree Ben stopped at the spot where he and the guys had slept. He sat on the hillside looking over the city. Various scenarios played through his mind. There was nothing that he could think of that would give Olivia a reason to break up with him.

When Ben arrived at the tree the owl was still there. She sat on her branch looking at Ben as if she was offering solace. It wasn't until Ben fell asleep that she flew off to hunt.

At school, Lilly walked over to Olivia in the girl's locker room during P. E. "What happened with you and Ben? He was so excited to get your call. When he got back he looked stomped on."

Olivia sat down on the bench. "My dad doesn't want us going out."

"Why not? He always seems glad to see Ben at church," Lilly asked puzzled.

"It's all a show," she said with embarrassment. "He thought Ben and I were just friends. You know that guy, Brad, living at our house? He found a letter I was writing to Ben and showed my dad. My dad really believes that races shouldn't mix. He says it's in the Bible."

A bemused look appeared on Lilly's face. "Wait, so you can't go out with Ben because he's not white? Did you tell him that?"

"Would you have?" Olivia asked.

Lilly stood stunned watching Olivia walk away, weeping.

After the break up, Ben became the ultimate hermit. He returned to his sanctuary, the sea, for comfort and asked for extra shifts at work. Anything to keep his mind occupied. His friends attempted to hang out with him, but Ben rejected their offers.

At the beach one weekend, Kenny, Dennis, and Jack were surfing. Jack saw Ben sitting on his board out in the line-up and paddled over to him.

"Hey, good to see you," offered Jack.

"Hey, Jack," returned Ben.

They sat bobbing in the waves. Jack couldn't keep quiet any longer. He knew why Olivia had broken up with Ben, and so did the rest of the group. Lilly had let it slip one night when they were trying to figure out what was up with Ben. Jack decided it wasn't fair for Ben not to know.

"Dude, I have some info for you, but it's gonna mess with your head. Wanna hear it?" Jack asked.

"What? She's going out with someone?" Ben responded.

"Naw, man. I think Olivia has become a nun. She doesn't even talk to guys, but I do know why she broke up with you," Jack shot back. "Her old man doesn't want her going out with you"

"Will?" "He likes me. Why would he do that?" Ben asked

"Yeah, as long as you're -- and I mean you, Ben -- aren't dating his daughter." Jack explained.

"What's the problem with us going out?" Ben asked. "How does that change how he feels about me?"

Jack hesitated, and then he just laid it out. "I'm sorry Ben, this is going to hurt, but you have a right to know -- it's because you're not white."

Ben paddled away and caught the next wave in and left the beach.

CHAPTER 29

How is it that every DJ on every radio station knows when people break up and plays songs that rip your heart out? Ben turned off his radio. He was stuck. Every song reminded him of Olivia and everywhere he went were places he had gone with her. He was constantly being made aware that he'd been dumped.

The most effective therapy for his devastated heart was the time Ben spent in the tree and in the water. One provided solace -- the other allowed him to burn off some of the frustration and anger that raged through him. Ben surfed with abandon -- with no regard for his safety. He took off on waves that he had no right being on. Some waves left him gasping for air after getting pounded on the shore. Other waves solicited hoots of victory at having dared and won.

It was only in the water that Ben had ever experienced true justice. There it was all choice and consequence. If he chose well, the ride was his reward. If he chose badly, the body slam on the shore was the result. At least the ocean gave him a choice. With

Olivia the choice had been made for him. There hadn't been an ounce of justice in that. Lying under the canopy of the oak Ben had spent numerous nights venting to the Almighty. He needed a face he could see to talk to, and thought of Joyce.

On the way to Joyce's house, Ben thought about the day he had met her. The necklace she had given him lay in a box he called his 'atta boy,' box. Ben had placed it there with the other special notes, letters, graded school papers, his varsity letter, and other tokens of success and affirmation that had been given to him. The box had been with him since his days at St. Margaret's. He'd been adding to it beginning in first grade. The item that meant the most to him in the box came from Rodrigo, his best friend at the Home. The stone was from White Sands National Park. Rodrigo and Ben had been climbing the white dunes when, there at their feet, was a jet-black stone. Both of them reached out to grab it and resulted in them knocking heads. Rodrigo ended up with the stone and treated it as a talisman. From then on, any time something good happened, he attributed it to the black stone. As the two grew older and began playing baseball, Rodrigo would rub the stone hidden in his trouser pocket while he waited to bat. The first year, he batted 450 with 120 runs batted in. In the years that followed, he became a little league legend. He and the stone had been inseparable until he gave it to Ben as a good-bye gift. If only the benefits of the stone had transferred to the new owner. The stone lay powerless, but greatly cherished in the box.

Ben pulled the piece of paper with Joyce's address written on it. He parked Lee's car into the driveway and walked to the house. He was about to knock on the door when he heard, "Ben!"

Sitting on the on the porch catching Joyce up on what had gone on since they had last seen each other put Ben at ease. The conversation flowed easily and amicably. It was obvious that Joyce was glad to see him, yet Ben was having a difficult time bringing up the main reason he had come to see her. He wasn't in the habit of trusting adults or even seeking their advice. Once he had left his uncle's house, he relied on only God and himself. Why Joyce had come to his mind when he decided he needed a face to talk to, surprised him. Here he was though and he might as well fill her in.

"I was going out with this awesome girl. When out of nowhere I got torpedoed and it was over. She picked me up at work a couple of months ago and told me that she couldn't go out with me anymore. I haven't seen nor talked with her since."

"I'm sorry to hear that Ben -- did she say why?"

He looked away from her and said, "she didn't tell me, but my friend did. My girlfriend's dad is a big dog in the church. He made us break up because I wasn't white. I never knew I was a minority until I started going to church."

"Ben, come here," she requested. "Give me your hand, see that?" "Fools like me pay hundreds of dollars and endure spray booths and all kinds of insane treatments to have skin, your color. The man who tried to belittle and devalue you is a little man. What you need to know is the church doesn't always work. It's full of us pinheads, but God always works. You'll see. Remember, God doesn't waste our pain. I know that probably doesn't go a long way in healing your heart, just know that time is a healer and a revealer. It may take awhile, but eventually we heal, and we discover why some of the crazy things we endured or were denied, happened. I said, some, not all. Some things will never make sense and will appear to be without reason. You'll be OK, and you'll be a lot smarter. I'm sorry for your pain."

Joyce was right -- the talk didn't heal his heart. He continued to struggle with the hurt and fester with anger. Some days he could pull it together, some days he couldn't. He had no choice but to cling to Joyce's words and hope that time would heal. One bit of practical advice Joyce gave Ben was to dump the hermit lifestyle. The advice sounded solid, so he called Don and asked him to gather the guys at A's for burgers. It had been months since they had all been in the same place at the same time. He felt like a kook for having avoided the guys. Ben hadn't meant it as a slight, or in a mean way -- he'd been harpooned through the heart and had done the only thing he knew to do when life came crashing down, which was to cocoon. Accordingly, he anticipated an uncomfortable reunion.

What Ben had forgotten was that he had true friends. They had given him the gift of space without casting any trips on him. When he was ready, they figured he would come around, and he did. At A's, they gorged on burgers and mounds of zucchini fries. It was a feast celebrating friendship, and Ben's emergence from his tomb.

The reconnection also included getting back together with the group that Ben had been hanging around with before his self-imposed exile. With it though came attending events that Olivia participated in also. At first Ben inquired if she was going to be there, but in time he just accepted that possibility and decided he would deal with it. At school he had taken routes to his classes that he knew she would not be taking, which also changed. Ben knew he couldn't go on living like she didn't exist. It hadn't been her choice or her fault that their relationship had ended. Maybe they could get back to being friends and at least be able to hang out in that capacity.

Ben also decided to go back to church. Although he didn't have any understanding about why the mess had all happened, he had a realization that it probably wasn't going to be the last time his skin color would work against him. The last shred of innocence that had remained from his upbringing in the Home was now gone. Skin color mattered. It would open or close doors for him. He would be accepted or rejected using the same system. Ben wondered why Ken and the guys had never made an issue of it. Was it a generational thing? Maybe Olivia's dad couldn't help himself. He had just been brought up that way. The man was living out what he had received from his father and from his father's father, and others before them.

Lying in the tree one night Ben made the decision to visit Olivia's dad. He had to try to understand where Will was coming from so that he could bring closure to it all. He was about to knock at the Higgins's house when the door opened. A startled Mr. Higgins stood speechless. Ben reached out his hand. "Hello, Will, I was wondering if we could talk."

The man invited Ben in where they sat stiffly and in silence looking at each other. Ben wondered if Olivia or Mrs. Higgins were home, but the quietness that filled the house told him that it was just Mr. Higgins and himself.

"Would you like something to drink?" Will offered.

"No thank you, I'm good." Ben replied. "I came over to let you know that Olivia and I have not been seeing each other as you instructed, not even as friends. I also wanted you to know that we never planned to run off together as Brad told you. She would never do something like that to you guys and I wouldn't have asked her to."

Will shifted in his seat. He looked like he was trying to gather his thoughts and come up with some kind of response. When he did, without looking directly at Ben, he said, "You're a big man, Ben. Someday when you have a daughter you'll understand. I know that I've hurt Olivia and no doubt you too, and I'm sorry about that, but I stand by my decision."

"Should I torch the man?" I"s he serious?" Ben wondered.

Ben opted for grace. He stood up to leave. "No, Will. I'll never understand your decision or your reasoning. If I ever have a daughter, she'll be able to date members of your race, and any other race." With that, Ben stood and walked to the door. As he left the house, he turned his head to look back and saw Mr. Higgins watching him walk away. After the visit, Ben also had the answer about whether he and Olivia could hang out as friends. The answer was no. It would only cause friction between her and her dad. He would be cordial when he was around her, but as far as it was up to him, he would not spend time alone with her. The closure he was seeking didn't happen. He still felt angry and devalued. Despite his bravado and the in your face response to Will he had accomplished very little.

CHAPTER 30

In the middle of senior ditch day, graduation pranks, and the celebrations, there is the realization that May is the season of endings for high school seniors. It is the accumulation of the unavoidable losses of adolescence they had experienced in the four years. The capstone is graduation, which would put a stop to the daily gathering in the classrooms and hallways of the school. Although most would not admit it, uncertainty was the prevailing emotion in the hearts of students. Despite the frustration and anxiety caused by the rigors of education, there had been a sense of comfort in the structure that school attendance provided. The last bell would soon ring and the students would be tossed out into the world forcing them to make critical choices.

Ben was sitting by himself in the senior mall when Jack and some friends walked over to him with an open yearbook.

"Ben, check out your senior prophecy, you're going to be a saint!"

Lilly grabbed the book and read, "Ben Storm will become a missionary and get the world saved."

Everybody started cracking up and teasing Ben who was fully enjoying the joke. "Yeah, right, they were probably thinking of Billy G. or better yet, J.C."

The gang continued browsing through the yearbook making comments and reminiscing. Watching the gang shot Ben back to when he had first met everybody. He remembered arriving at Middle School feeling like an alien, and how Katy had helped him find his classroom. There was also the time Ken and the guys gave him some of their clothes so that he didn't have to wear his lame, parochial school uniform to school. He had made the transformation from hick to being slick because of his friends. Foremost among his memories though was the time he had spent living with Don and his family, and Dave and his. Ben thought about the times when the quiet man's rage was so intense that he barely made it out of the apartment. He remembered walking to Ernie's house and tossing pebbles at his window in the early morning hours. Ernie would come downstairs to let him in so he could have a place to sleep. Sitting on the wall that day in the senior mall with his friends, Ben was overwhelmed by the deep love that he felt for them. So much had happened in their lives. Choices were made that would result in sobering consequences, or launch them into various stages of success. One thing was for sure though – all of them had been changed.

Soon, they would all disperse to various places. They would be scattered across the U. S. Some would be going off to college, others to the military, and some would stay in town. This reality was the ultimate unavoidable loss of their waning adolescence.

Two weeks after that afternoon at the senior mall, with great fanfare, laughter, joy, and sadness, the senior class walked across the stage and into their imminent adulthood.

After graduation, Ben asked Lee for a couple of weeks off. He had stashed away enough money to take a trip to the Hawaiian Islands. For the past year he had been planning out his stops among the different islands -- Oahu would be his main focus. Ben was studying a brochure when he thought he heard footsteps. He instantly froze and listened. He looked over at the owl and saw that she too, had heard the noise. It wasn't like the person was attempting to sneak in. The footsteps were loud and purposeful. Ben crouched down lower behind the tree branch so that he had a better view of the path leading to his tree. He knew that once the person crested the small hill that dropped into the grove, he would know what action to take. When he saw who it was though, he was at a loss. Ben was prepared for confronting strangers, animals, fire, lightning, and numerous other scenarios, but he was not prepared for this.

"Ben? Hello?" The girl slowed her walking and called out softly again, "Ben?"

"Olivia? What are you doing here? How did you find me?" A puzzled Ben asked.

"Don't get mad. I told the guys I really needed to talk with you and they told me how to find you. They weren't sure if you had already left for Hawaii. I took a chance hoping you were still here. Why didn't you tell me you didn't have a place to live? All the time we went out and I never knew."

"Nobody knew until I told the guys. I've had plenty of places to live, and surfed many couches, things just never worked out.

Then I found this tree. It's been home for some time now. Why are you here?"

She walked closer to the tree, "I wanted to see you. Can I come up?"

Ben hesitated. Her coming was a bad idea. He had closed that chapter, or at least he thought he had. He had told her dad he was not seeing her, yet here she was. His brain and heart were sparring. One said to be a gentleman and walk her back to her car, and the other was yelling, *"Fool! Are you serious? Here she is!"* Heart won.

"Sure, come around to the other side. I'll drop a ladder."

Once in the tree, Olivia sat next to Ben amazed. "You did all this? How did you even find this place?"

"I didn't really do much. The way the branches are formed made it easy to make it a living place. I added the tarps and other comforts. Anyway, God led me here when Dave's folks divorced. I was out of options, and He gave me all this. Come meet my room-mate." The owl glared at Olivia, but willingly took the strip of raw meat from her hand.

As evening came they lay on the lounge chair pad holding each other. When the stars came out Ben moved her head closer to his. "Look up. See all those pinpoints of light coming through my ceiling of green? The nights that I can't sleep I try to count them all. The most I've ever counted is 345. It never fails to put me to sleep."

"Can I stay here tonight? I brought my sleeping bag."

Ben sat up. "What about your folks?"

"I told them I was spending the night at a friend's house. You're my friend right? And don't worry . . . it'll all be innocent. I leave on Friday. My dad got transferred to Chicago, and I want my last night in California to be with you."

Ben knew that after this night he would never see her again. He climbed over to where he kept his spare lounge chair pad and laid it down on the branch across from his. Tonight he would not be counting stars, and there would not be sleep. He and Olivia talked, cried, and laughed, and then talked, laughed, and cried some more. The owl left to hunt leaving the two alone. In the morning Ben placed his flannel shirt on Olivia to stave off the chill and walked her to the car. After a long embrace she stepped into her car and drove off. Ben started the long walk back to his tree. Neither of them dared to look back at the other. Olivia turned up the radio and pushed down the accelerator on the T-Bird. "Good-bye Ben Storm. I am so going to love you for a long, long time."

CHAPTER 31

Ben's plans to go to Hawaii didn't work exactly the way he had planned. The gang had been hanging out at the beach when they decided to get some lunch. Katy and the girls headed over to George's for avocado and cucumber sandwiches, the guys opted for burgers and smoothies. Ben noticed a sign in the window of one of the shops. It had a guy dressed in Navy dress blues standing next to an old time warship. "Join the Navy and See The World," it beckoned. "You guys go ahead, I'll catch up," Ben murmured.

By the time Ben came walking up the sidewalk they were all done eating. Jack handed him his lunch. "Where'd you go?"

"I think I just joined the Navy," Ben answered.

Everybody cracked up at Ben's joke. "Yeah sure, you in the Navy, and I'm gonna be an opera singer," teased Katy. They walked back to the beach and returned to their towels to make the most of the sun's rays. Ben closed his eyes, confident that he had made a wise choice.

When he returned to the oak, he spent the next couple of days packing his stuff, taking down the tarps, and returning the tree to its original condition. He walked through the grove to make sure he was leaving it as he had found it. Then he went to work.

Driving around the town delivering his pizza's made the shift fly by. Ben was no longer washing dishes so he spent very little time in the restaurant, which made it hard to talk with Lilly. He was hoping to catch her after work, but found out that she was working a short shift and would be gone long before he got off. He would talk with her the following day. He also planned to turn in his two-week notice to Lee and end his time of employment at Graziano's when his shift ended.

Lee's decision to hire him had saved his life and he would be forever grateful. The job had provided income, food, and for a time, shelter. It had also provided him with Lee's friendship. In four hours he would give his notice and then in two weeks it would be but memories.

After his last delivery Ben and the staff cleaned up and prepped for the next day. When they were done they punched out and left leaving Ben alone to check the doors, the stoves, and ovens, and close the restaurant. It was 1 AM when he turned off the Open sign and locked the door.

When he arrived at the oak he sat under its great canopy on the branch next to his packed bags waiting for the owl to return. He knew she would arrive just as the tip of sun broke the horizon just like she had done hundreds of times before. The owl glided silently and landed next to Ben.

"I'm moving out," he told her. You know I'd stay here forever if I could, but I can't. I gotta do what I must do, until I can do what I want to do. Thanks for sharing your tree and for all the great talks. Well, at least for listening. You take care, dear friend."

The owl stared intently at Ben. Its brilliant yellow eyes searched his face for more information, but that was all Ben had to offer. She watched as Ben grabbed his gear and left, dragging the lounge chair mattress behind him. When Ben had walked a ways from the tree, she left her perch and followed him until he reached the end of the field. The owl flew two circles around him and then returned to the safety under the canopy of the oak.

Ben walked to a pay phone and dialed Lilly's number. "Hey Lil, is your offer still open? I moved out of my old place."

"You mean your tree?"

"How'd you find out?"

"How do you think? Don't freak, we haven't told anyone. Didn't you ever hear the guys at your tree? They've been taking turns checking on you ever since they found out you were rooming with an owl."

"Umm, I'm feeling a little bit lame here. Well, anyway, I need a place to stay for a couple of weeks."

"Of course. You can come over after work."

Ben thought that it was the pink walls of the room where Lilly's sister used to sleep that were giving him insomnia. After lying awake for hours he got out of bed and went to the garage and grabbed his old lounge chair mattress. He quietly opened the door leading to the backyard and lay down under the big cottonwood tree, listening to the familiar music of the night. He was asleep in minutes.

Two weeks later, Ben boarded a bus for the Navy Recruiting Depot in San Diego. He would be going to Hawaii and to places he had only dreamt about or looked at in the pictures of Surfer magazine. He was going to the Western and South Pacific . . . except this time it was going to be a guided tour. "Jesus, Mary, and Joseph!"

Part 2
EIGHT YEARS LATER

"Ben, everything that has happened in your life to this point, I mean . . . St. Margaret's, your dad, you living in that tree, you raising yourself, your Navy stuff, our time at college -- God's going to use all that. You're ready for this. Relax and go to sleep."

Annie,

CHAPTER 32

There was a BMW full of teens waiting for the light to change as Ben pulled up. The driver glanced over at the 1962 VW van with surf racks on top, and motioned for Ben to lower his window.

The kid pointed at the rack on the van roof. "Are you lost? Ocean's about 1700 miles in that direction," he snickered.

Ben smiled at them. He lowered his head as if he was looking for something on his dashboard while keeping his eyes on the light. When it turned green he hit the gas and left the Beamer behind him. The startled driver revved up the sports car and quickly caught up with Ben.

"Surf's up, dude!" Mocked the teens as they raced past him waving, 'hang loose,' gestures from out of the car's windows.

He continued to cruise through the town, thinking back on all the cars he had beat off the line while waiting at intersections. In the end, they always ended up racing by him, but he loved the sound of gears grinding and tires squealing as they attempted to recover their pride at having been beaten by a VW Microbus.

When he arrived at his destination, Ben turned on his blinker and turned into the church parking lot. He was about to park when he decided to do a drive-by and scope out the facility and grounds. The church was located on a corner with a residential community around it, and commercial and retail sites across the street. All around the church were huge fields of grass. Whoever had picked the location had made a wise choice.

Ben parked the van and walked onto one of the fields. From there, he looked back at the church. The building looked like it had been built sometime in the 70's. Its design was modern and looked like at capacity it could hold 500 people. As such, the facility was smaller than his youth facility at his prior church. Still, it had potential.

"Well, let's go meet the people and see the inside."

There was an elderly secretary sitting at the desk typing at sonic boom speed. When she didn't look up to acknowledge Ben, he walked closer to the desk.

"Hi. I'm the new youth guy. My name's Ben."

The secretary barely looked up and pointed to the wall that showed an arrow pointing down to the basement, labeled; Youth Room.

"All-righty then, excellent to meet you too," Ben called back as he headed down the stairs.

The basement was just that. A space composed of several storage rooms, one of which was used by the youth group. After looking around he found another set of stairs leading to the main floor and went exploring. He was excited to see that the sanctuary was a multipurpose room with basketball hoops and markings on the floor for two basketball and volleyball courts. This was a definite plus. The design of the building and the surrounding fields said to Ben that someone had been thinking of kids when they bought and developed the property. There wasn't much flash to it, but it was very practical. It would do.

Later at his apartment, Ben sat in his living room and looked over the list of youth volunteers that he had inherited from the previous youth staff. They were a mix of twenty-somethings, married, and unmarried, -- most were without kids of their own. Some of the staff attended the local university. Perfect, thought Ben. "Hope they really love teens."

He called each of them and invited them to meet him at a local restaurant that weekend.

When the day arrived, Ben walked in to see the gang gathered around the table. He did a quick visual assessment looking for battle fatigue, or burnout. The youth staff was probably doing the same with him as Ben walked toward them.

"Thanks for making time to meet with me, I know it was short notice. Would you like something to drink?"

In time Ben was relieved that he has sitting among a staff that was experienced, friendly, and hilarious. He did sense though that they were tired and frustrated. He spent much of the time listening and memorizing their names and how they were connected. Ken and Tracy had been helping out for three years. Kurt and Molly were dating, Sam and Bill were still in college. Of the group, Ken was the most vocal.

"It's getting old just entertaining kids," Ken volunteered. "We've either been scaring the hell out of the kids, guilting them, or doing crazy crap to get them to take the Bible serious and come and bring their friends!"

Elissa jumped in with, "I think some of the kids get it, but over all, I agree." "It's like we're always scrambling to find the next big thing that's going to explode our numbers," added Tracy.

Kurt had been sitting quietly listening to the conversation. "Some of the kids seem burnt out or have been hurt."

Ben had met kids like the ones the staff were describing before. They sounded a lot like some of the kids he had worked with in California, mostly the church kids.

"Youth group is on Wednesdays, right? What if we push back youth group and do an event instead -- a party, like the party Matthew threw for his buddies."

The staff was intrigued. "What type of party?

Ben was about to share his idea when Ken stood up and left the group. "I'll be in the car," he said to his wife. "I'm not feeling well."

Sitting in his car, Ken's face clearly projected the disappoint-ment he was feeling. He had been hoping that the new guy would focus on making disciples. His mind went into overdrive. "What's up with youth pastors and their fun and games? This Cali guy is going to be just like the rest."

After the meeting Tracy walked back to the car. "You need to give Ben a chance. Just cuz he likes to have fun doesn't mean he's shallow."

CHAPTER 33

With the help of the staff and a team of parents, the gallery of the church was transformed into an airline concourse. Parents behind the visitor's booth acted as ticketing agents checking kids in. A huge sign hung over the entrance of the gallery that read: Mahaloa Airlines.

Eventually a bus pulled up made up to look like an airplane minus the wings. Teens boarded and took off. Elissa and the staff walked the aisle passing out peanuts and soft drinks. After a short ride the bus "landed" at a shopping center where parents were waiting in cars marked to look like taxis. They quickly placed the teens in various cars and whisked them off to the Luau.

When the teens arrived, they were amazed at what they saw. The place looked like Maui, complete with hula girls who were busy placing leis on the teens. In short time the students were either dancing, swimming or porking out to the amazing spread of island cuisine.

Ken had been supportive but guarded. He mainly stayed in the background and watched. What he couldn't ignore was the amount of preparation, thought, and work that had gone into this event. Ben had wanted to create something that the kids would be proud of, and included their parents, and fun. He wanted to create space for the kids to play and pray. It was obvious from the sounds and the looks on the faces of the teens that it was working. He saw Ben and Annie standing by themselves and walked over.

"Ok. I'm sold, but we're going to do a devotional or something at the end, right?"

Ben placed his arm over Ken's shoulder. "This whole thing is the devotional, Ken. We don't need to work in something spiritual. Joy is spiritual, so is fun. Look at them. I read just the other day in Romans that the Kingdom of God is all about righteousness and peace and joy in the Holy Spirit. I'm seeing some of that here. C'mon! Let's dance!"

When the classic song, "YMCA," came on, that's all it took. Ken grabbed Tracy and sauntered onto the dance floor. Soon he was leading the YMCA cheer.

That week some of the youth group kids were sitting around at lunch talking about the event. They commented on what a cool gig it had been and about all the new people they had met. Their consensus was that it was not too shabby, but that it had been weird seeing the staff dancing. The most encouraging statement was that it was just cool to see everybody having a blast.

CHAPTER 34

The first year rocketed by. There was so much energy and a huge sense of excitement around the youth group. The numbers of youth volunteers were up and the students were bringing their friends.

Ben had just walked into his office when he noticed a note on his desk. He closed his door and dialed the Senior Pastor's number, then walked to his office.

Frank was sitting behind his desk wearing the same light blue Hawaiian shirt he had worn the day Ben had been hired. He remembered thinking that Senior Pastors who wore cool shirts couldn't be all uptight. It helped in his decision to accept the job. Frank stood up as Ben came in.

"Hey, Ben. Thanks for coming in. How are things?"

He relaxed a bit and shook Frank's hand. "Good, Frank, what's up?"

The pastor motioned for Ben to sit. "I had this letter given to me last Sunday. There's no signature but the writer appears to be representing a group of our parents. You haven't received any calls or letters have you?"

"No. I get calls from the kids but haven't heard from any parents." Ben replied. "Why?"

Frank picked up a letter off his desk. "Here, read this."

Ben could feel his ears get hot and his heart begin to pound. After reading it, he handed the letter back.

"They're upset at all the non-Christian kids hanging around the church?" "Seriously?"

"Sounds like they're also upset that you're ignoring our church kids and spending more time with the others," Frank commented. "You aren't right?"

"Frank every school day the staff and I take a church kid out to lunch. I speak in their classrooms, and meet with them after school."

The Senior Pastor walked out from behind his desk and sat down next to Ben. "That's all I need to hear. Don't worry about it. If people don't have the guts to sign their letters it sounds like sour grapes to me. You'll be dealing with this as long as you're in ministry. I call 'em snipers. Let it go, and keep taking care of those kids."

Ben took the long way home hoping to decompress. It didn't work. He pulled into his driveway just as Annie was getting home. She leaned out of the car window and yelled, "winner by a bumper!"

"Loser cooks dinner!" Ben sat in his car holding the letter. Anne walked over. "Dang, you don't have to be a sore loser."

He handed Annie the letter as they walked into the apartment. "Somebody gave this to Frank last Sunday. I just got done meeting with him." He left her reading the letter and came back dressed in sweats and a T-shirt. "I'm going for a run."

After running countless laps around the track, Ben lay on the grass with his eyes closed. When he opened his eyes, he saw Annie sitting next to him.

"I thought I might find you here. Doing OK?"

Ben rolled over on his stomach. "I'm getting that bumper sticker."

"Yeah, which one?"

"Mean People Suck! Better yet, I'll get the tattoo."

Annie pulled Ben off the grass. "HA! Come on, race you?"

They shot off running like the wind and neck to neck until they got to their driveway. Annie gave it an extra effort and beat Ben by a full stride.

"That's twice in one day. You owe me a burger."

Ben sat across from Anne watching her reread the letter. He remembered the first time he had seen her in the cafeteria at the college they were attending. Later she showed up at a bar he was playing at. He had been immediately smitten. How he had managed to get her attention continued to amaze him. Yet, here she was, married to him and sitting across from him nibbling on her hamburger while she tried to make sense of the letter.

"There's no signature. Frank know the person who gave it to him?"

"Naw. He was cool about it. He said not to worry about it. I bet he gets letters like this a lot, calls them snipers."

"I bet he does," Annie replied. "Teachers get these too. They always make it sound like they're representing thousands of people, usually -- it turns out to be 2 or 3 max. Frank's right, let it go. You know how to handle snipers, don't you?"

"How?"

In her best impersonation of Yoda, Annie clued Ben in. "Clear shot must you give not, to snipers."

Ben tried to keep a straight face. "Yes, Master Yoda."

CHAPTER 35

No matter how strongly Ben tried to dislodge the letter and the feelings attached to it from his mind, they kept ambushing him. This usually occurred while he was driving, or working at his desk. It reminded him of the time when he was checking in at his first duty station while in the Navy.

He had been granted a twenty-four hour pass before he had to report to the U. S. S. Midway, docked at North Island in San Diego, CA. Ben figured he had enough time to do a quick visit with Lilly and his friends so he asked his shipmate to drop off his sea bag at the ship for him. His friend, however, ended up getting arrested in Tijuana and put in jail, so Ben showed up at the ship wearing a pair of jeans and a T-shirt from a surf shop.

He was escorted to the Medical/Dental compartments where he met the rest of the crew he would be working with and the Chief who was in charge. They were all having a great time getting to know each other. One of the guys offered to show Ben to the berthing area. As Ben turned around to follow him, he heard the chief trying to pronounce the word on the back of his T-shirt.

"Ma-ran-tha?" "What the hell does that mean and what's with the dove?" he smirked.

Ben turned around and said, 'It's Maranatha.' "It means the Lord is coming."

The Chief let loose with a string of profanity, and mockery. "Not another one of those!" Ben heard him say as he walked away.

From that day on, he was a kook. 'One of those.' He'd been judged without any more information other than what had been written on the back of his T-shirt. The snipers at the church were no different. He was deep into his pity party when the youth staff showed up.

Elissa handed Ben a burger and a soda. "So, I hear we got some fan mail."

"Yes, yes we did. No big deal, just a worried parent, but that's what parents do right?" "Worry? Guess we ought to allow for that. I mean, look at our bunch. We've got a rep from every youth cultural and social group represented. I'm talking jocks, preps, nerds, skaters, grits, punks, mods, and wavers. Then there's Luna who could very well be from the moon."

"No big then?" Inquired Ken.

"I don't know. Should I be worried?"

"I don't think so, just don't get cocky," advised Tracy.

Ben reached for another burger. "Right on then. Let's plan summer." The chalkboard in Ben's office was soon covered with numerous options. The ranges of choices were varied. One of the choices beamed out at Ben -- a road trip.

"Let's go west. Let's do an old school music and drama gig and take it on the road. This group is loaded with talent. We can see if we can book a stop at the Native American Mission where our Compassion International child lives. I also have some contacts in Arizona, and California. There's even a chance we can get down to Baja, Mexico. I think the experience could be eye-opening for those of us living in the choice city."

"We're not doing the 1970's polyester leisure suits and brides-maids dresses thing, right?" Mike asked. The response to that was a collective, "Yewwwwww!"

For the rest of the meeting, the crew listed everything that had to happen, and what they would need to pull off the trip. The biggest item on the list was to find a Greyhound type bus and buy it. Nobody had any ideas for where the money to buy the bus would come from. It would take hundreds of car washes to raise $14,000. Regardless, the meeting continued on as if that issue would take care of itself. Ben assigned tasks to the staff members, and assigned some to him. The summer Spirit Sound, trip was on.

The first thing Ben did was to design a poster of the bus they were looking for which showed the bus in pieces. There were lines attached to a bus part so that the people of the church could sign up to buy a tire, the steering wheel, or a whole side of the bus. He placed it in the church gallery and announced the trip and told the church how to get involved the following Sunday. Then he contacted Earl, a retired school principal and coach.

Ben immediately liked Earl. He had first met him when he drove the students to their first camp. The man had an easy laid-back manner about him and smiled all the time. The kids loved him. Even better, Earl could not only drive a bus -- he could fix it. Before he called him to set up a meeting, Annie and Ben prayed long and hard that he would agree to help Ben find a bus and become their driver.

Earl had heard about the trip and had even signed up to buy of all things, the drivers seat and steering wheel. The meeting was almost too easy. Earl agreed to help Ben find a bus and be the driver for the trip. Eventually, Earl would go on to drive the bus for the next five years that Spirit Sound toured the Southwest.

In the next week Ben called the Navajo Mission in Cuba, New Mexico to see if he could bring Spirit Sound down to do some repair projects, meet Bernie, the kid the youth group was sponsor-ing, and put on their show. He called a college in the San Diego area to reserve some dorms for the kids to stay while they were in San Diego. He also called friends in Albuquerque and some in Phoenix, Arizona to arrange some places to stop and sleep on the way west. The last call he made was to an organization in San Diego, California who took youth groups into Baja to build houses.

That night at dinner Annie looked over the plans that Ben had come up with and the contacts he had made. "Looks like we'll be making three stops before we hit the coast." She was about to ask another question when the phone rang. It was from the director of the organization with the house-building project. Annie heard Ben seal the deal, and thank the lady. He walked back into the room with a huge smile on his face. Everything was jelling nicely.

In the inner city of San Diego a lone, young black girl sat on a swing in an otherwise empty park. Out of nowhere, a car lunged into the parking lot. The doors flew open and a body was thrown out. Moments later, the police swarmed around the park. In the midst of the commotion, the little girl slipped quietly away.

In the same part of the city a young couple, Pete and Julie, lived two blocks from the park. On that day, they sat finishing their lunch. The noise coming in their window from the event at the park was a noise they were very familiar with. The couple had been living in the area since they graduated from college and had been doing ministry with the house building organization and within a church where Pete served as the youth pastor. They were going to be critical partners with Ben, the staff, and the students in Spirit Sound.

Pete was about to go outside to check things out when the phone rang. "Yeah?" "Hey, Fay."

After hanging up, He went to the kitchen and looked at Julie with a bemused look on his face. "Fay wants me to bring some kids from Colorado into our hood to do an inner city project at a park or something, and into Baja to build a house."

Julie took the piece of paper with Ben's number written on it. "Tell her we need to know more. Besides the park is booked 24/7 by the thugs."

Pete seemed intrigued. "Could work. I'll call the bro, see what he's thinking."

CHAPTER 36

The youth staff, Annie and Ben stood staring at the bus poster on the wall in the church's gallery after church one Sunday. It was as if they hoped that by doing so it would magically increase the number of sign ups to buy pieces of the bus. The poster had been up for over a month and it contained only 25 signatures. At this rate, the deadline would not be met and Ben would have to resort to chartering a bus, which meant the price of the trip would go up. The staff worried that if the price went up some of the kids might have to drop out due to the cost.

It was a somber staff that was about to head out the doors when Lee walked up. One of his sons had been in the youth group and Leeland had always been supportive and encouraging. "How much more do you need to buy the bus?"

Ben pointed to the poster. "We still need eleven grand."

"Go find your bus." I'll mail a check to the church tomorrow." Leeland smiled at the stunned staff and casually walked away.

The staff looked at each other with huge eyes. They walked out of the church wondering if they had heard Leeland right. When it hit them that they had, they ran screaming like Banshees across the fields until they ran out of energy. No one dared to talk as they lay on the grass staring at the sky. It was too good of a moment to interrupt. They had the money and now it was up to Earl to find them a bus.

"Jesus, Mary, and Joseph!"

"Earl!" Ben shouted in the phone. "We have the moola . . .Yes, seriously!"

Two weeks later Ben drove to an industrial part of Denver to meet Earl. When he pulled into the lot he saw numerous over the road type buses, but no Earl. Ben continued walking around checking out the buses. He rounded the corner and saw Earl standing next to a bus talking with a salesperson.

"Hey Earl, is this our bus?" Ben asked as he introduced himself to the agent and was about to board the bus.

"Nope." "Our baby is right over there," pointed Earl.

Ben turned around to see a classic 1972 MC-7 Gray Hound bus shimmering in the noonday sun.

Earl thanked the man and told him he would be calling him. He placed his arm around Ben's shoulder and led him to the bus.

"This is ours?" "Does it run?"

"Listen to this." Earl jumped into the driver's seat.

The engine worked hard to engage, smoke began billowing out of the pipes. Finally the engine settled down and began to purr. Earl and Ben look at each other and broke out into huge grins.

It took a couple of weeks to make some small repairs on the bus and spruce it up. When it was ready Earl drove the bus to the church and picked up Ben. They cruised to a burger joint where Ben had asked the staff to meet him at one of the outside tables. The classic MC-7 pulled up, air brakes venting, and with Earl giving a blast of the bus's air horn that rattled the restaurant. The bus door opened. "Get in!"

The rest of the day was spent with Earl driving the staff all over the city and up into the foothills. When he parked it back at the church nobody moved. They knew a miraculous event had occurred before their eyes. It was if the seats of the bus had become pews in a mobile sanctuary and everyone sat with heads bowed offering up quiet, reverent filled thanks for a man named Lee. They now had the means to get to all points west and the great unknown that lay before them.

CHAPTER 37

He wasn't kidding when he told the youth staff that the youth group was loaded with talent. Ben walked into the gym to watch the students prepping for the production. The singers were working on a song, the dancers were going through a number, and the actors were busy with their skits. He watched as Molly walked from group to group checking in and offering suggestions. When she saw Ben she told the girls to take five and walked over.

Ben was clearly pleased. "Dang, they look awesome. Great piece."

"Cheri and Jen choreographed it," she remarked. "Is every-thing OK?"

"Everything's fine. I just wanted to get a feel for how things are coming."

Molly pointed to the various groups in action. "Chill, it's moving along great. Look at them. We'll be ready."

As he was leaving one of the students called out to him. Ben looked back to see Byran walking towards him. His usual care-free facial expression was missing. Earlier in the week Ben had been having lunch with some of the students. Although they seemed excited there was also a sense of apprehension that could be felt. The students had expressed concerns about them being white and going into multicultural communities. They were also concerned about the unknown. In addition, they had tons of questions. Fear was probably at the top of the list.

"Show's going good. Sure this is still a good idea?" Teased Byran.

"Absolutely Byran. Why are you asking?"

"Just checking. Taking us white kids into the jungle sounds crazy to me."

"Hey, we're not all white. I'm red. We have some color!" Ben jokingly shot back. It's not the jungle. I'm thinking it's gonna be good for you guys to see how the other side lives."

Byran wasn't letting it go. "It'll all be good until the girls can't use their curling irons and stuff."

"Dude, we're not going to the outback, and you better be careful talking like that. I've been on campouts with you guys, and I know these girls can hold their own. If Beca and TJ had heard you, you'd be on the ground right now getting nuggies pounded into your skull," warned Ben.

Byran had to laugh. "Hey, just saying. We like comfy."

Ben noticed Jon standing in the gym watching the students re-hearse. He had only been coming to the youth group for a month. He had a gentle manner and was well liked by the kids. Nobody had invited him to youth group he had just shown up one night and kept coming after that. Ben walked over to him.

"Hey, Jon." Ben said.

"You guys are really going to Cali?" Jon asked.

"Yeah. We're taking our show on the road . . . coming?" I think there's still some room," Ben offered.

"I don't do church and stuff. We used to, but since my mom died we stopped going." Jon volunteered. "Can I still come?"

"I'm sorry to hear about your mom, Jon. You don't have to come to our church to come on the trip. Come up to my office and I'll give you the papers you need to fill out and get signed."

Jon basically lived as an emancipated youth. His dad was al-ways on the road and had given Jon a credit card to buy the ne-cessities of life. Most of the time Jon was alone in a large custom home in the nicer part of the city. He didn't have any siblings, but seemed to have a very active social life. Ben was glad he was sign-ing up for the trip.

"That does it. All we need is for your dad to sign off on these and it's a wrap."

The boy gathered the papers. "I really need to get outta this town, and it would be good for me to be around you guys. Thanks for letting me go. My dad gets back into town this weekend. I'll get the papers back to you at church on Sunday."

"Remember, you're welcome to come, but you don't have to attend our church to be a part of our youth group," Ben reminded Jon. "Although, I'm excited to have you as a member of our production crew."

Jon reached out his hand to shake Ben's and closed the door behind him. The boy left leaving a sense of a burdened spirit in the room. Despite his mellow manner, there was a heavy countenance about him. Ben sat thinking about all the teenage latch key kids he was meeting in this affluent town. He reflected on a pas-sage he had recently read; *"Seeing the people, He felt compassion for them, because they were distressed and dispirited like sheep without a shepherd."* The youth staff and Ben spent large amounts of time acting as surrogate parents to many of the youth. Ben had lost count of the number of times he had taught a kid to drive, and get their driving license. He made a personal commitment to spend time with Jon, and hopefully get to know his dad.

CHAPTER 38

The next few months saw the staff and students alike scrambling to get things done. The departure day was rapidly approaching and there were still a number of loose ends that had to be tied up. There had been several changes to the production as new parts were added or replaced. All the connections that had to be made were completed. Ben had spent numerous hours on the phone with Pete and others connected to the trip. Overall everyone's spirits were still high and the excitement level was rising. He was grateful to have such quality staff members working with him. The student's parents had been so helpful and supportive. In the middle of the commotion and activity there was so much joy and celebration.

Ben followed up on his commitment to hang out with Jon. Although he didn't skate, he'd go to the skate park with him and shoot footage of his skating ability. The conversations that came up during these times were revealing and enjoyable. Jon wasn't the only one benefiting from these times. Ben began to look forward to hanging out. Being at the skate park allowed him to meet other students and in time he started to develop some moves of his own on the concrete. It wasn't like being on a wave, but it was close. The wipeouts however were much more painful.

In time the meetings became less frequent. Jon informed Ben that he had found a job and would be working most afternoons and evenings. He did plan to request Wednesdays off so he could attend youth group and the practices for Spirit Sound.

Ben was nursing one of those wipeout wounds when the phone rang. Frank wanted to know if Jonathan Moore was a part of the youth group. The pastor was asking because he had gotten a call from Jon's dad.

"Hey, Frank. Yeah he just started coming more consistently. He's going on our summer trip."

These meetings had the same feel and Ben was expecting to hear about an unhappy parent, but instead, Frank asked him to meet him in his office. Annie noticed his concerned face. "What was that about?"

"I don't know. Frank got a call from Jon's dad and wants me to meet him at his office. He gave her a quick hug and grabbed his car keys. "I'll be back."

Frank's car was the only one in the parking lot when he arrived. Ben parked next to it and walked in the building. He knocked softly on the office door.

"Ben?" Come in," invited Frank.

He walked in and waited for the pastor to speak. His grave appearance told Ben that he was either in big trouble, or that Frank had something really heavy to tell him. "Jonathan's dad found him in his room this morning. It appears that he overdosed. His note said something about some drug deal gone bad."

Ben remained standing holding the note and looking at the Senior Pastor. He had no words. His heart sank -- his mouth tasted of bile. He was sure he was going to vomit. The pastor went up to him and led him to a chair and placed a cup of water in his hands.

"I'm sorry, Ben. Jonathan's dad said that his son thought highly of you. He called because he wants you to officiate his son's funeral. I'm sorry to spring this on you with the trip coming up and all. Let me know how I can help. Here's his number."

Frank walked out and let Ben sit and try to collect himself. The door to the building echoed as it closed. The only other sound that could be heard was a terrible wailing emanating from the Senior Pastor's office. After a long while, Ben picked himself off the carpeted floor and walked to his car.

Annie had been waiting by the phone. She heard footsteps coming up the stairs to their apartment and ran to the door to let Ben in. She could tell that whatever had happened was bigger than a sniper situation. She wrapped Ben up in a huge embrace as he began to weep.

"Jon killed himself." That's all that Ben could manage to say.

After some time, they sat in the living room talking between tears as Ben filled her in on the details.

"I need to take a walk, is that OK?"

Ben left and walked through the perfectly appearing neighborhoods. When he got to the high school football stadium, he climbed the tall observation light poles and climbed into the baskets overlooking the field. This was a place where he went when life turned hard, he was feeling stressed, or needed to think. Today, he wasn't sure what he needed, but he knew that he needed it in large amounts. He began to pray.

"I needed to get as physically close to you so that you could really hear me because I so need to hear from you. In two days I'm going to hear all kinds of cute platitudes, and clichés about how Jon is in a better place, how you must have needed another actor, etc . . . at the funeral. The truth is that a young vibrant man, who was trying to find a better way of living, is dead. The other truth is the officiant, me -- who's supposed to bring some solace to the grieving needs your touch -- right now!"

While Ben was praying, a piece of paper floated out as Ben opened his pocket Bible and landed on his jeans.

"Ben, the God I know, doesn't toy with us, and He will never waste our pain. Somehow, pain will always have a purpose, like some sort of preparation, maybe."

That note had been given to Ben so long ago. He reached into his T-shirt and pulled out the necklace that Joyce had given him. In that moment, sitting high above the football field, Ben felt a presence he had not felt in a long time. It was the same presence he had felt the day he was walking in the field behind Dave's house after his parents had divorced, and the same presence that he had felt among the oaks. He knew he was now going to be on his own, but that he would be all right. Perhaps it would be the same in this situation.

Once he was home, Ben sat in his favorite chair. Annie sat on his lap and clung close to Ben marveling at the vastness of the resources of their God as he carried them, calmed them, and filled them with His strength. Ben would honor Jon and speak of him as a brother and a friend.

CHAPTER 39

Jon's death impacted Ben deeply. The day before they were to depart for all points west he was sitting in a circle at the gym visibly still shaken. Ben tried to conduct the necessary meeting to make sure the group was ready to go. His questions fell on the floor without registering with the group. It was a terrible, hollow silence that filled the gym. The longer they sat in stillness in the gym, the more the tension grew. At long last Caleb ventured a thought, "maybe we should scrap the trip? Maybe your friend's death is like a sign."

That single statement opened the emotional gate and a torrent of words, and sentiment flooded out.

Byran stood up and walked into the middle of the circle. "I don't know about that, but I mean, here I am getting ready to go off and sing and tell people about God and I'm not even sure I believe in God. Especially after this."

Others began to chime in. A wave of uncertainty engulfed the room. Some in the room began to weep.

The overall consensus was that they wouldn't be able to pull off the production. They acknowledged all the progress they had made and were confident in their creative and performance abilities. All of that though, had happened within the safety of the gym. It was going to be like being in another country once they left the choice city.

Ben let the teens process and share their fears, concerns, and thoughts for a long time. He had been pacing as he listened. When there was a prolonged silence he spoke.

"Yesterday, I wanted to scrap the trip too. I wanted to quit my job, school, and move to Maui. Not today. This is our chance to do something that we will remember for the rest of our lives. Bus leaves at 6:30 AM. I hope all of you are on it. However, if you decide to stay, I will give refunds."

He was about to dismiss the meeting when Becky stood up. Normally, Beca would have contributed numerous comments. She had been sitting with her head in her hands the entire meeting.

"I have no idea why things have happened the way they have, but I know one thing -- God doesn't toy with us, and he will not waste this pain. Ben, you need to do this for Jon, for God, and we need to do this for ourselves."

Ben looked up at her shocked. The words she had just spoken were the words that Joyce had written to him eight years ago! He walked over to her after the meeting.

"Beca, the stuff about God not toying with us, where did you get that?"

"I'd been praying this whole time. It just came to me, and I felt compelled to share it," she said.

That night Annie and Ben lay in bed discussing the meeting in the gym. Annie was attempting to reassure him. "They'll show up. They're just a little nervous. I would be. You need to hang on to what you said to the kids about this being a chance to do something that all of us will remember for the rest of our lives."

When Ben continued to rest fitfully, Annie sat up. "Ben, everything that has happened in your life to this point, I mean . . . St. Margaret's, your dad, you living in that tree, you raising yourself, your Navy stuff, our time at college -- God's going to use all that. You're ready for this. Relax and go to sleep."

5:00 AM flashed across the alarm clock's face. Ben and Annie were out the door in forty-five minutes. They saw that Earl had the bus parked in front of the church, but there was no sign of him. They had just made the decision to wait in their car for him to arrive, when they saw him heading their way from the church. Anne and Ben walked over to meet him.

"Hey kids! I'll start her up so she'll be warmed up for the road. We're still leaving at 6:30?"

Ben glanced at his watch. They had about 15 minutes to go. "Yep, that's still the plan. We're going to get some coffee while the bus does her thing. Would you like some?"

"You kids go ahead. Earline set me up with a full thermos."

Annie and Ben were almost across the street when some cars began to turn into the church parking lot. They turned and walked back.

The parking lot was soon full of activity as parents dropped off kids, turned in forms, and helped pack the bus. Ben acted as if this is exactly what he had expected. He had hoped the students would choose to go, but there had been some doubt and he had mentally prepared himself for disappointment. Annie came up to him as he was checking the roster. "So, doubting Thomas, what did I tell you?"

With a blast of the air horn the bus pulled out of the parking lot and the adventure began. Excitement and uncertainty floated through the bus as the students settled in for the long ride.

CHAPTER 40

'WELCOME TO NEW MEXICO -- THE LAND OF ENCHANTMENT', beckoned the sign as the bus left Colorado and entered the outskirts of Raton, New Mexico. Earl pressed the air horn as they crossed the state line. The students had been either sleeping, reading with their headphones on, or talking with each other. Now, everybody was awake. Entering into New Mexico energized them even though it would be another five hours before they would arrive at their first destination.

For the next two days, Spirit Sound would be making small repairs, cleaning, painting, and performing for the staff and the residents of the Mission. It was easy to feel that they were the noble benefactors. The students were bringing their talents, giving of their time, and leaving the comforts of home. They oozed altruism, or at least they thought they did. In short time there would be a major reversal of roles. The paupers would become the wealthy, and the gifts they would give the students would be anything but the expected. By the time the bus was packed again, lessons would be learned, hearts would be softened, and personal agendas would be placed on the shelf.

The loud hissing of the bus's air brakes attracted a crowd of Navajo children. When it stopped, Caleb pulled the lever to open the door, and jumped out.

"YO, little dudes!"

The children saw Caleb's prosthetic leg and took off running. They eyed him suspiciously from behind a tree. Byran quickly pulled his window down.

"Dude, get back on the bus! You're scaring them!"

Caleb jumped back on the bus as fast as he could. The children had run and hid behind some trees and were talking among them-selves. They were trying to figure out what or who Caleb was and why his left leg was made of metal.

The windows on the right side of the bus were all pulled down and the students crowded around to watch the drama being played out before them. From where they were they could clearly hear the conversation between the children. They were arguing among themselves and making guesses about the strange being they had seen hop out of the bus. One thought he was a pirate, another was sure he was a robot. They ended by daring each other to board the bus and find out. Some fighting was occurring over who should go, when a girl who looked to be about four pushed her way past the guys heading toward the bus.

"Marcella! Get back here!"

Marcella stood at the open door of the bus with her hand on her hips. "Robot. Come out!' She demanded.

Nobody knew what to do. Caleb moved away from the window and looked at Ben.

"Robot, I believe you're wanted outside."

The teen hobbled to the door and walked over to the little girl. He stood waiting to see what she was going to do. After looking Caleb over she reached out and touched his metal leg.

"Where are you from, Robot?"

Caleb looked at the bus and then at the little girl. "Uh, Colorado."

The little boys that had been hiding behind the tree, mustered up the courage to come out from hiding. Caleb started doing a robotic dance to the delight of the kids, and in that moment became the star of the kids at the Mission. He couldn't go anywhere without a group of kids following him. With that as an icebreaker, there was a mass exodus from the bus. Earl sounded the bus horn bringing out the Mission staff and many more of the kids living at the mission. Ken opened the bays of the bus and started a working party to unload the gear, suitcases, sleeping bags, pillows, and everything else they would need for the time they would be at the mission.

The director of the Mission was a quiet elderly individual who had a quiet serene spirit about her. It was very evident that the staff of the Mission and the kids loved her. Ben quickly picked up that she ran an efficient and effective ministry.

He followed Mrs. Simpson into her office along with Kurt and Elissa to get her insights, get some instruction on the culture of the Mission, and of the Navajo people. Initially, it was hard for the staff to focus on what she was saying because they were so taken with her Irish accent. She let the staff know what was proper and improper behavior that the students needed to pay close attention to. As the meeting concluded, she handed Ben a list of the repairs that needed to be done. Mrs. Simpson got up.

"Thank you for coming, Ben. The children and teens have been looking forward to this. You'll find everyone here very loving and kind. You also need to know that Bernie, the boy you sponsor lost his brother in a car crash last week. He may be a bit standoffish. I would let him approach you."

With that she was off in a flash to oversee and manage her domain. The staff lingered in her office marveling at the women. They had so many questions about her and her background. They perused the galley of pictures gathered on the top of her piano of the many children she and her husband had adopted over the years. There were so many stories sitting on top of the vintage Steinway. All they knew about Mrs. Simpson was that she had been a widow for 30 years and that her husband had been a mis-sionary pilot. How she happened to be the director of a Navajo Mission in Cuba, New Mexico, had to be a great story. It was a long way from the savannas of Africa.

CHAPTER 41

After living on fast food since they had left Colorado the students were grateful for the steaming plates of pinto beans and rice. The warm chewy fried bread was an exceptional treat that the students heaped with butter and honey.

Ben looked around for Bernie and saw him sitting with a few friends. While most of the kids of the Mission had found a student to sit with, Bernie and his friends were sitting away from people. He decided to do a walk by to see what kind of response he'd get. Ben was about to head in their direction when he noticed a boy sitting by himself.

"Mind if I sit with you?" He asked.

The boy shrugged his shoulders and moved over. Ben took that as a sign and sat down. After brief introductions they moved on to making small talk and discovering things they had in common. While they were talking, the boy saw his big brother coming to his table.

"Time to go Martin," ordered Bernie.

Of the kids to sit next to, Ben had chosen the right one. How could he have known that he was sitting with Bernie's little brother? Martin was about to pick up his tray and go with his brother.

"Bernie?" Inquired Ben. "I've been wanting to meet you."

Martin broke out into a wide smile, "You know my brother?"

It was obvious that Bernie felt uncomfortable. He shifted his weight from foot to foot and looked away from the two. Sensing this, Ben decided to close the conversation and wait for another opportunity.

"I enjoyed getting to know you, Martin. Thanks for sharing your table with me."

He smiled at Bernie, and walked away. Ben was grateful to hear Martin making positive comments about him to Bernie, and about their talk. Perhaps the encounter would pave a path to making a connection with him.

In time the Mission's gym was transformed into a performance hall. The show was in process with the final scene coming up. Ben went back stage to talk with Molly just as the girls on the dance team walked by dressed in what he considered to be seductive.

"Molly, they're not going on like that, are they?"

They're leotards it's what dancers wear." Molly replied,

"They're showing too much skin. We're going to offend these people. Tell them to go put their T-shirts on."

Clearly frustrated Molly walked off to talk with the girls. The instructions did not go over well.

"Seriously?" Challenged Jill.

"Yes. You're going to have to put your T-shirts over your tank tops."

Molly was about to leave to tell the students in the act before them to stall for as long as they could so the dancers would have time to make the change.

"No way! We're going to look like dorks. We're not doing it. What's Ben's problem?"

Molly was in no mood for a power struggle and she knew they didn't have the time for this. Ben would just have to pull rank and make it happen. She found him pacing at the building's entrance.

"They're not budging and won't dance if they have to put t-shirts on."

Ben angrily started off to talk with the girls. When Molly grabbed his arm.

"You need to seriously consider your words to those girls. They've worked hard for this show. They're outside."

Ben found the girls looking hurt, but defiant. He was about to let go on them, when Molly's words caught up with him. He had intended to come off confident and authoritative, but instead stammered as he began to speak. "I, uh,"

The girls quickly interrupted. "What are you embarrassed about?" Demanded Cheri. "It's not like we're hanging out of our clothes!"

He looked at the girls. Ben had known many of them since they were in seventh grade. They all had good hearts. Molly was right. The girls had worked hard. He dropped the power guy mojo and shared his concern.

"I think if you go on like that, we're going to offend these people. They're very modest -- we need to respect their culture."

A silent standoff ensued. Both sides had millions of charges and counter-charges racing through their brains ready to be volleyed as needed. Ben looked at his watch.

"You guys are on in five minutes. You have a choice to make."

Ben joined Annie in the stands as the lights dimmed for the final act. She had no idea what had transpired outside. The production was going off well. The familiar introduction to the girls dance came on. Ben held his breath. The girls had made their choice. One by one, they danced onto the stage with the T-shirts on over their Danskins. They had found a way to make the T-shirts fashionable, yet reflect modesty. The show ended to thunderous applause.

The following morning as the students were working on various repair projects, Cheri and the girls saw Ben working by himself and went to talk with him.

"Hey," Cheri said shyly.

They started talking at the same time attempting to restore their relationship. After a couple of awkward attempts, they started to laugh.

"Are we good?" Ben questioned.

"We're good," they chorused back.

Ben felt relieved. He had not slept well having spent the night ruminating over his decision to have the girls wear the T-shirts. One trait that he did not want to be known for was being legalistic. He had experienced enough of that in the time that he had been a part of the Christian community. He had not wanted the girls to feel like they were being judged. In the end they had made their choice based on their sensitivity to the Navajo children and the Mission staff. It was a decision way beyond their years.

While the students were packing up Ben went to a spot he had designated as his prayer corner. He glanced up and noticed some of the students with Bernie standing in the cemetery next to the Mission, and around a grave. While he had worked so hard to reach out to Bernie, the students had connected teen to teen. They had included him in their basketball games, shared their music, and just hung out. On this day, they were grieving with him at the loss of his brother. Ben may have had the title of professional minister, but for the past two days it had been Spirit Sound who had been doing the pastoring in so many capacities and situations.

Earl did a final walk around, locked the bays, and yelled: "All aboard!" The Navajo children took that to mean them too and piled in. It was a while before the staff could pry the children out of the student's arms. When the staff was sure everyone who didn't belong on the bus was off, they gave Earl the go ahead. The air brakes made a hissing sound and the bus started to move. Ben sensed something was up when he noticed the grins on several of the student's faces. His hunch was right. Just as the bus was passing past the Mission's gate, Bernie and Martin walked out of the bus's bathroom. Earl drove them into town for burgers, and then headed back to the Mission. It set them back an hour, but those last moments with the brothers cemented a relationship that had in the past consisted only of a picture, and monthly letter updates about Bernie's progress and activities at the Mission. They were bonded from this day on. The bus stopped at the Mission gate, and Bernie and Martin stepped out like big dog celebrities to the admiration of the rest of the Navajo children who had come running once they saw the bus. Then with a blast of the air horn that sent the children scattering Spirit Sound departed out for destinations west.

CHAPTER 42

The MC-7 bus zoomed through Arizona. The group made a quick overnight stay removing only sleeping bags, pillows, and toiletries. At 6 A.M. the next morning staff had everybody up. By 6:15 A. M. the bus was on its way to California.

Ben called the staff to the back of the bus for a meeting. He also wanted to give them a chance to offer ideas, evaluate the trip, or vent if needed. It was the first time they could meet for an unlimited amount of time since they would be on the road for the next six hours. The conversation was highly animated. Ideas shot out like rockets. There were some feelings of frustration over not being able to have spent more time at the Mission. Other than that the staff was pumped. After the two-hour meeting they called it a wrap.

Annie went up to her seat behind Earl. She had declared herself the official, 'I will keep Earl awake while he drives,' guard. Ken waited for the staff to go back to their seats. Then walked over to Ben's seat and hovered. When it was apparent that he was not leaving Ben asked, "what's up, Ken?

Ken slid in next to Ben. He ran through several ways to say what he had been feeling since they had left the Mission. Eventually, he blurted it out. "Look, I was sure we would have had some major malfunction by now like it has on other youth trips I've been on. Maybe it still will, I don't know. What I do know is that something special is happening here that none of us could have programmed. It's almost scary. I mean the way the girls handled the situation at the Mission, how amazing the students were, the fact that we staff are energized when we ought to be exhausted, it's not normal."

Ben waited to see if Ken was going to say anything else, but he went into a silent deep thought mode, put his headphones on and listened to music while glancing out of the window. In time, he dozed off with a smile on his face. Throughout the bus the students were in great spirits as the bus moved along the highway. When Ken woke up, he went back to sit with his wife. Ben was about to take a nap when Byran sat next to him.

"Don't you ever have doubts about this God thing?"

"Do you mean have I had all my questions answered? Ben replied. Bryan hesitated before he answered. "Yeah. I guess. I just want to know if you have always been this God dude." The 'God dude,' remark cracked Ben up. "That's the first time I've been called that." He went on to share about his upbringing at St. Margaret's and how he had served Catholic Mass from the time he was six. Ben also told

Byran that he had walked away from the faith of his youth and remained that way until his senior year of high school. Some of the kids overheard the discussion and joined the guys.

"Back to your question, though, I still have many questions floating around in my noggin. Mostly about the church though, the organization part, and I wonder about how many times the way we Christians sometimes seem to be our own worst enemy." Ben admitted, "I found my faith and almost lost it all in high school."

The discussion soon turned into a question and answer session. What most of the students wanted to know was what had happened during Ben's senior year that almost turned him from his faith.

Ben reflected back. "To be truthful, I almost walked away from my faith a couple of times. The most serious was toward the end of high school. My friends had finally talked me into attending church. It was at church that I first experienced prejudice and dis-crimination. Until then no one really made a deal about me being brown, red, or whatever I am."

"They didn't let you attend their church because of that?" demanded Byran.

"Naw, it wasn't like that. I started going out with this girl that I met there, and her dad didn't want her going out with me because I wasn't white," Ben explained. "It rocked me really hard. After that I wasn't sure if I wanted anything to do with church or Christians."

The students were so into the discussion that they missed the sign welcoming them to California. The only way they knew was that Earl had blasted a notice with the air horn. There was a brief acknowledgment from the teens then they returned to talking with Ben. The students were livid. They began to share stories of their own concerning similar situations that had happened to them or their friends.

"Bro, I would've just said, see ya," remarked Caleb. "That is just so wrong."

The girls wanted to know about Ben's girlfriend. They began to talk amongst themselves about what they would have done. Ben hadn't meant to stir things up or cast a poor image of the church, but it did. The positive outcome was that it made the students think about how they had been coming off to their friends at school and at home to their parents who were not Christians.

"How come you never told us about this before?" Byran asked.

Ben wanted to bring some type of closure to the talk. "I didn't think it was important, and no one had ever asked. Besides, all of that is in the past. Here's what I want you to know: The church, the institution part, doesn't always work. What I know for sure and I can tell you with all of my heart is, that God always works. He always does."

The students went back to their seats and continued to talk. The talk had triggered many topics. A break through of sorts had also occurred. As a result of the talk the students no longer saw Ben as the cool Cali guy with the good-looking wife and who seemed to have it together. He was just like them -- only a few years older with more life experience than they had. He carried pain, bore emotional scars, struggled with questions, and was doing his best to live life and to live it well. He had allowed himself to be known, and now they in turn could open up to him.

Annie put Ken in charge of the Earl watch and went to sit with Ben. She could tell he was tired and talked out, so she guided his head onto her shoulder and let him sleep.

CHAPTER 43

T he Ocotillo trees and sand dunes of southeastern California were long behind them. U. S. 8 changed from two lanes in either direction to eight. The first thing Ben noticed was the palm trees . . . the unofficial iconic symbol of California. He marveled at them standing tall and stately against the setting sun. The first time he had seen the trees they were swaying in the wind as it rushed through the neighborhood of his new hometown. That had been a long time ago.

Ben had planned to live three years max in Colorado and then return to the coast, but Annie had fallen in love with the Centennial State. As a result he had been landlocked like the boat he once passed as he drove across the plains of Eastern Colorado. He remembered that he had almost veered into on-coming traffic as he looked over his shoulder to make sure he had really seen the boat. Driving on, Ben realized that he and the boat were brothers, each feeling the other's pain . . . each of them out of place. Now at the first sight of the towering Mexican palm trees, Ben knew he was again in the land of the sun and the shore.

The sun was on the horizon as Earl eased the bus into the entrance of the college where Spirit Sound would be staying for the next week. He parked along one of the dorms. Although the students were tired, they quickly unloaded the bus and settled into their assigned rooms. Ben ended up sharing a room with some of the guys and quickly fell asleep.

Once Ben was asleep Caleb decided to pull a prank on him. He had developed a remarkable skill after much practice that enabled him to wag his stump. Because of Caleb's athletic ability and his strength, getting hit by his wagging stump hurt badly. Maybe it was because he was weary from the many hours spent on the bus that caused Caleb to make the poor decision to stump a sleeping Ben. He stealthily inched closer to him.

Brandon hissed out a warning. "Dude! Don't, he'll go ballistic!"

Caleb quietly hopped over to Ben's bed and positioned himself next to Ben's head. He looked over at the guys with a sinister smile then started stumping Ben. Although he was in a deep sleep Ninja like, Ben reached out and grabbed the first thing his hands fell on. He gave it a hard twist and knocked what he thought was an intruder to the ground. "Ow, my nose!" wailed Caleb.

Realizing it was Caleb -- Ben eased off and released his hold. "Do you have a death wish? I could've killed you," he yelled. Ben turned on the light to reveal Caleb moaning and gingerly cradling his quickly swelling nose while the rest of the guys sat wide-eyed in their bunks. "You broke my nose," Caleb sadly announced.

Ben walked over to him. "You're good. It's not broken; let's patch it up." After Ben turned the lights out the room was bathed in silence. It was so quiet in the room that the usually gentle soothing sounds of the crickets coming in the open windows sounded as if they were screaming. From that night on, no one ever messed with Ben when he was sleeping.

At dawn, a strange sound began drifting down the dorm hall-ways. At first the sleeping students thought the sounds were a part of their dreams. Some woke to glance at their watches to see that it was only 6:00 AM. The sound turned to chanting with an African rhythm and then singing began. Doors began to open as Ben and the staff walked down the hallway singing along to, "The Lion Sleeps Tonight." Exactly at 7:00 AM, Ben rang the breakfast bell and students started coming out of the dorms. Caleb came out of his room with a huge bandage on his nose. He was not happy, but much wiser. For of his playfulness, and joking manner, Caleb was a serious and deep thinker. Ben and the students marveled at his ability to ski better that them all with only one leg. In addition, he had participated in numerous long distance bike rides to raise money for Cancer Research, many of those over elevations of 10,000 feet. Caleb did more with his one leg and prosthesis than most people did with their two good legs.

During breakfast the students seemed pensive. Although they sat in groups of eights they had all retreated into a personal space. The bowls and plates before them seemed to have pulled them in the way that a campfire does. In an hour they would board the bus and cross the border into Baja. For most of the students it would be the first time they had left the U. S.

Ben thought back to the meeting in the gym the night before they had departed from Colorado. There had been so much uncertainty and fear in the room. He wondered if those feelings were resurfacing and made a mental note to assign someone to stay back in case some of the students couldn't make the trip either through sickness or fear.

After breakfast the youth staff quickly got the students packing the bus partly as a distraction to some of the anxiety that was floating in the air. After the bus was packed Ken divided the group into two groups and started a quick game of Capture the Flag. Before long the mood of the group changed. They wearily climbed aboard the bus and they were off. The bus joined the excruciating crawl of cars waiting to cross the border. It was a flurry of humanity with street vendors and Federales walking up and down the street. Street vendors swarmed the bus. One of them hopped on the hood of the bus and began to clean the windows. Others lifted flowers, chewing gum, and ceramic pottery at the windows as they pitched their wares.

"Keep your windows rolled up," Ben cautioned. "We'll have a day of shopping later in the week."

Whatever fears the students were struggling with, were now gone. In its place was a deep fascination of the carnival type atmo-sphere that engulfed the bus. At the same time the harsh reality of the prevailing poverty peeking out from the street corners and the alleyways of the town struck them.

Earl turned the bus and headed east to the city of Tecate. The road ran parallel to the U. S. -- Mexican border leaving the thrill of the city behind them and with the blandness of the desert surrounding the bus. The sun blasted the bus with the steaming Sonaroan desert heat that began to affect the air conditioner on the old MC-7. It was working as hard as it could -- still, inside the bus the temperature was rising.

Ben had been in a similar situation before on another trip. He called the staff to the front of the bus and laid out a plan in case the air conditioner gave out. He had Earl pull over so the staff could pull one of the coolers out of the bays. Once they were back on the bus, the staff began passing out bottles of Gatorade to each student. Ben advised them to sip, not guzzle the drink. He then re-gathered the staff up front so they could talk to Earl while he drove. Looking at the map, it appeared they were only fifteen miles from the work location.

"What do you think Earl?" Ken asked.

Earl looked up at the rear-view mirror at the students. He looked out at the desert and the road before him. The heat bouncing off of the asphalt made his mind up for him. "I'll tell you this, we don't want to breakdown here. Let's make a run for it. Open the windows and I'll put the pedal to the metal," he advised. At the sign declaring the distance to Tecate, everyone ex-haled in relief. They were only three miles away. Soon small adobe houses began to show up along the roadside. Eventually, the town came into view looking very much like Tijuana, but smaller. Earl eased the bus into the first gas station he saw and set the brakes. The hot interior of the bus had put people's patience to the test. One of the parent sponsors, Lynnette, came over to where Ben was sitting. "Who are we supposed to meet here?" she fumed.

Ben was a bit caught off guard. She was normally sweet and mellow. He casually replied, "oh just some Ramon, he's supposed to be watching for our bus."

That wasn't good enough for Lynnette. She huffed off the bus and headed to a group of men standing by the store next to the gas station. "Which one of you is Ramon?" "We've been driving forever in this heat, and we need to get to the church." The men looked at each other. They could tell she was look-ing for someone named Ramon, but since they didn't speak English they hesitated to reply. Lynnette stood waiting causing the men to realize the woman was not going away without an answer.

Annie watched with concern the standoff-taking place at the store. "Ben, go get her!" "She really thinks we're meeting a guy named Ramon."

Ben called Ken and some of the other male staff who spoke Spanish and headed off to call Lynnette off the guys. First they apologized to the men, and then pulled Lynnette aside. The staff stayed behind to talk to the men. When Ben had walked her back to the bus, he said, "Lynnette, haven't you ever heard us calling each other, Ramon?" "There is no real Ramon -- it's just what we call each other. I don't know how it started, but what I meant when I said some Ramon was meeting us, I meant just some guy."

Lynnette's face began to turn red, Ben readied himself for an explosion, but then a sheepish smile spread across her face. "Oh," was all she said, and climbed back on the bus.

Before long a van from the organization they were there to help pulled up. A jovial, 40ish man with a well-rounded abdomen stepped out and with great excitement walked over to the bus. He showered the staff with hugs and handshakes and treated them like they were his long lost relatives.

Pastor Enrique Hernandez summoned up the help Earl needed to fix the cooling system and had them on the road in an hour. After a brief lunch, the teens were hard at work sifting sand to make mortar so they could add stucco to what would be the Pastor's new church building. Everyone labored hard under a merciless sun long into the day. There was no complaining and everyone was doing their part. Before long they had two sides of the church completed.

"All right, let's wrap it up. You guys are amazing. Look at what you've done!" Ben praised them.

The students were wiped out. They admired their work and then quickly began cleaning up and replacing the tools where they had found them. They had done what they had come to do and had done it well. Another youth group would be there the following week to complete the church. Pastor Hernandez came over beaming and appreciatively shaking each of the teen's dirty hands. Then he asked Ben, "Do you think they could do a song or something for the people?"

Ben scanned the sweat-soaked, dirt-caked faces of the teens and called Molly over. "The pastor wants to know if we'll do part of our show for them."

"Here -- now?" "We don't have our sound tracks," she informed him.

"I hate to tell him no," Ben replied. "Could we do a couple of tunes, acapella like?"

To her credit, Molly called Spirit Sound together, and there on the dry sun baked dirt that would serve for a stage they joined hands and sang. They didn't stop there. The students continued with their show and performed like they were inside a grand con-cert hall before a crowd of grateful and gentle people.

It was a long quiet ride back to the dorms. When they ar-rived the silence continued. The students walked into their rooms, closed their doors and fell quickly asleep. Ben and the staff walked to the bluffs overlooking the ocean where they too, had difficulty finding the words for what had happened that day. They could have ended the trip right there and it would have been enough.

CHAPTER 44

Annie and Ben rose early to run. They ran past huge athletic fields, along the bluffs overlooking the Pacific, past classic bungalow type buildings turned into classrooms, and the most amazing landscaping. They had just rounded a corner when they saw the entire Spirit Sound crew sitting on the grass in a circle. They had decided they needed to talk about their day in Baja and had gotten up and dressed hours before the wake-up call.

One of the guys was sharing as they neared the group.

"I was thinking. I mean, I just realized yesterday was Sunday. We worked on a Sunday instead of going to church. Then I thought wait, I'm doing church! What we did yesterday was church. I don't know if I can ever just sit in a pew and do that, 'stand up, sit down, repeat after me,' stuff again."

After he spoke various voices joined in. One of the students who had been grilling Ben over his faith stood up in the middle of the circle. "Gotta say it. I was not having the greatest time. I was shoveling that sand and thinking, I paid to do this? Then I looked over and saw Jill, Cheri, Megan, and Cindy working on the wall, and I looked at the face of the pastor just beaming. First I felt like a jerk, then, I just started grinning like a fool. I haven't felt joy like that in forever."

Ben and Annie kept walking. This space and these moments belonged to the students. Some of the students began to weep and move closer to each other. One of the dancers spoke through her tears.

"Yesterday on that dirt stage and smelling like a truck driver . . . for the first time in my life I felt so free as I danced. I've danced in so many recitals with huge stage sets, but it was always about technique and so scrutinized. Here, I just danced. I danced for God, those beautiful people and me. It was, I don't know. I can't describe it, but I will never forget it"

The sharing went that way until the breakfast bell rang. The students walked in groups to the dining hall. While they had been touched by the love and gentleness of the children of the Navajo Mission, the simple people of Baja had greatly moved them. It was as if each place where they ministered at had taken a slice of their hearts.

After breakfast Ben asked Annie to do a short talk to prepare the students for their next stop. They would soon be in another environment vastly different from their comfortable neighborhoods in Colorado.

Standing at the front of the bus, Annie began. "One of my favorite writers is this guy named Dietrich Bonhoeffer," listen to this. *'I should like to speak of God not on the boundaries but at the center, not in weakness but in strength, and therefore not in death and guilt but in man's life and goodness. God is the beyond in the midst of our life, and the church stands, not at the boundaries where human powers give out, but in the midst of the village.'*

"So far this week you have danced and sang and toiled before the very face of God, first in New Mexico, then yesterday, right in the midst of that little Mexican village. Today we'll be at a park where we will spend the week hanging out and loving on the people of City Heights."

Caleb leaned over to Byran. "Could get sketchy from here."

The students sitting around Caleb heard him and looked at each other anxiously. Byran gave Caleb a shove. "Dude!"

Caleb's statement set an apprehensive tone that wafted through the bus. No one spoke. Earl steered the bus off the freeway and onto the off ramp. He slowly drove through a neighborhood of 1940s' era homes with metal bars over the windows and doors. The students' faces were glued to the windows of the bus. They were taking in every detail. Finally, he stopped the bus at a park.

"Sure this is the spot?"

"Yeah, Pete should be here," assured Ben

Four black children stared at the bus as they walked to the park. They had seen plenty of school buses moving through their neighborhood, but had not seen anything like the classic MC-7 over the road bus, and they had never seen so many white kids at the park before. Thirty-four anxious students peered out at the four little girls.

"We've got customers -- let's go!" Earl barked.

Ben was as unsure as the students. "Wait. Just four of you girls go out so we don't scare them to death."

While they were figuring out who should go out, Pete showed up and climbed in the bus.

"Hey Ben! Hello everyone," he casually called.

Everyone on the bus was still looking out the window at the children.

Pete wondered. "Well, are you guys getting out?"

Ben looked at him sheepishly. "Yeah, we just didn't want to scare them. What do we do?"

"Bro, they're little kids," Pete laughed. "Grab a ball, some toys and go say hello. I'm sure they're not packing guns."

Earl stepped out of the driver seat. "Give me a ball, let the grandpa show you how it's done. Come on, Annie."

Before long the students had crafts, games and snacks going. In time, a few more kids showed up. Some of the guys started a basketball game that attracted even more visitors. The plan was to be at the park for a couple of hours, but with the excitement, that plan was forgotten. The next time Ben checked his watch, they had been there four hours and were on the fringe of missing dinner at the college. Ken was about to set up the volleyball net when Ben blew the whistle and gathered the students and staff to the bus.

"It's a wrap, let's pack it up."

Nobody wanted to leave. What had happened at The Navajo Mission, and in Baja was happening here -- connection.

Annie walked back to bus holding one of the girls hands. "See you guys. We'll be back tomorrow so tell all your friends!"

The next day, the students woke the staff up. They were ready to go back to the park. Breakfast was rapidly consumed. The bus was loaded, and the students were in their seats. Ben and the gang walked leisurely back from breakfast. They were greeted by an impatient shout from the students.

"Hurry up!" "Let's go."

Earl rounded the corner approaching the park to find over a hundred kids waiting for them. A girl approached Annie, followed by fifteen of her friends. "You came back."

"Of course we did, silly," teased Annie. "What's your name?"

"Rosa Magnolia Jones. I'm ten. These are my friends and cousins, she replied."

"Miss Rosa Magnolia Jones, now that is one beautiful name. You brought all these kids?"

"Yes, Miss. They were scared at first, but they came.

"Why would they be scared?"

The little girl looked over at a parking lot. "Hardly no one comes to this park. See that bread truck over there? There's police inside."

Annie called Ben over. "Why? Do they know that you know they're inside?"

Rosa picked up some Play Dough. "Yes, It's because of the gangs. Yeah, they know."

"Well, come on missy. Let's go see what the kids have set up for you."

Annie dropped the kids off at an arts and craft table and walked away with Ben.

They stood looking at the bread truck. "If it's a police surveillance unit, we need to talk with Pete. I think he's at the gym."

Ken, Pete and some of the guys from Spirit Sound were having an intense game of basketball going with the neighborhood kids. Ben motioned to Pete.

"Pete, a word please?"

"What's up?"

"Why is there a police surveillance unit camped in a bread truck in the parking lot of the park?"

Pete looked a bit chagrinned. "Oh, that. Bro, every park around here has that going on. Welcome to gang central. There are a ton of drug deals going down around here. If you came to do inner city ministry, this is the place where it's needed.

"Are the kids safe?

"They're as safe as the children who have packed this place today. They took a chance coming here too. I've been living here all my life and this park has never seen this many kids at one time, but I could look for another place." Pete offered.

"I'll get back to you, thanks."

Ben and Annie walked out of the gym and back to the park. Everywhere they looked Spirit Sound kids were engaged in some activity with the children.

Annie joined them. "I say we stay" she called back to Ben.

The time at the park ended way before anybody was ready. Students began packing up, giving hugs and then piled on the bus. Earl had only gone a couple of blocks when one of the staff members yelled out. "Where's Tim?"

Mike called out, "check the John."

Charity pounded on the bus' bathroom door. When no one answered, Ben got concerned and walked up to Earl. "Let's go back to the park."

Earl parked the bus alongside the curb and opened the door. Ben, Ken and Mike hopped out and walked to where a group of kids were still gathered. Tim was sitting in the middle of the group showing the kids how to make lanyards.

"Uh, Tim?" Ken said softly.

Tim looked up from what he was doing. "Hey guys."

"Did you notice everybody else is gone?" Ben inquired.

Tim stood up and looked around. "Whoa!" "Where'd every-one go?"

Ken gave Ben an incredulous look. "Uh, on the bus. You're lucky Charity noticed you were missing."

"I was?" "I've been right here the whole time," Tim countered.

It was no use. This was typical Tim. He was much loved for his easygoing nature.

"Say good-bye and get on the bus -- Kook!" Ken ordered.

Tim walked onto the bus to cheers and sneers from the group.

Ben was not amused. "From now on we're going to count off before the bus leaves anywhere. Caleb, you're one. Count off."

The students chorused out their number. When the count got to Tim he sat unresponsive.

"Tim, you're sixteen." Ben called out. "Let's try it again. Go Caleb."

The next time when the count got to Tim, the entire group yelled out, "TIM!"

CHAPTER 45

Music echoed throughout the canyon-like walls of the school's outside corridors. It bounced off the concrete sidewalk and went careening into the air. Mixed in with the heavy bass and drumbeat, were the hoots and chatter of appreciative dance aficionados. Ben followed the smooth sounds of Bob Marley and saw the Cali kids mixing it up with the Colorado kids, taking turns stepping into the circle and showing off their moves. Although they were worlds apart culturally and geographically, they had found the language common to all peoples . . . music and dance.

Ben watched in silent admiration. He forgot that he had come to hustle the students off to prepare for their show that night. The music in that moment, mesmerized him, it froze him in time. All that mattered was what was occurring right then, right there. Had it not been for Annie coming to check on what was taking the group so long to get back to the school, Ben would have probably let the dance circle go on through the night. She walked past Ben and stood next to Beca.

"People, very cool, but you guys go on in like, 15."

The scene collapsed. The music shut down, but not the connections that had been made. The students grabbed a hand of their new friends and followed Annie and Ben to the gym where they had their friends sit in the front row seats that had been set up for the production. They'd been given the best seats in the house so that the same energy that had propelled them as they danced would extend to their performance on the stage. It was more than that though. They wanted their friends to be able to feel their passion and their reason for leaving their homes. The synergy was palpable. It was like humidity and it hovered over the space that the students and the neighborhood kids occupied. It was a stationary front of holiness.

As the Grand Finale of the show approached the fog that had been produced by the mixture of hot ice and water swirled on the stage. To everyone's amazement it began to lift. It floated above the stage and then began to drift out in the gym. The students had just concluded their last dance and were singing their final song. At the end they began to proclaim:

"Holy, holy, holy is the Lord God Almighty, who was, and is, and is to come."

"Holy, holy, holy is the Lord God Almighty, who was, and is, and is to come."

This refrain continued for several minutes. When the music ended the students ended up kneeling with heads bowed before what was meant to represent God's throne. No one in the gym moved. Not a word was heard. Then the crowd rose to its feet and let out a huge and prolonged applause. The members of Spirit

Sound stood and faced the audience with jet lagged like looking faces as if they had just returned from another place . . . a hallowed place far, far away.

Eventually, they walked back stage.

"Ok. Am I the only one that felt that?" Byran asked.

The silent nodding of heads affirmed that they had all experienced something powerful. Something that they could not put words to, but that they would remember for years to come. The students formed a circle and gave thanks, then went to meet their friends who had remained sitting in the front row. Amidst the excitement and the overflowing joy, the students told stories to their friends about how they had come to faith. The narratives were told simply without the trappings of dogma. They were told in the language and sincerity of youth. They were raw and honest, yet with sidesplitting humor. Ben took a lesson from watching the kids and wondered if that approach could ever work in the wider platforms of the organized churches in America.

Throughout the dorms that night students continued talking as they lay in their beds. The sense of awe and wonder prevailed. The realization that the next day would be their last day in California caused a solemn quiet. Sleep soon overtook them and each of their subconscious filled with dreams. It had been the most wonderful, eventful, very good, totally amazing, incredible day.

CHAPTER 46

Volleyball courts had been set up on the grass, across the field arts and crafts tables were placed, and snacks were brought out as they prepared to conclude their stay at the park. The place was packed with people. Ken and Tracy walked over to where Ben was helping some of the girls unwrap the ceramic pieces they had brought for the children to paint.

"Dude, we have rival gangs playing on the same volleyball court."

Ben put his hand up motioning for them to stop talking and led Ken and Tracy away from the kids. "Who told you that?"

"See that guy over there?" Tracy asked. "They call him, Shaker. He told me we better be ready for anything."

"I think Pete is in the gym. He'll know if the dude is telling the truth. I'll check it out," Ben reassured them.

"Pete!" Ben called out. Pete called in a replacement and went to see what Ben needed.

"Do you know the gangs around here?"

"Yeah," Pete calmly replied. "You've got members of two of the gangs playing volleyball, and some here on the court."

"Should I be concerned? I mean it's safe, right?" Ben asked.

"Naw, and yes we're good. They'll be all right. Besides, they've been here since Tuesday. Not an issue my friend."

While Pete and Ben were talking five cars of the Operations Unit of the San Diego Police Force pulled into the parking lot. An elegant female Commander stepped out of one of the cars. The officers watched for a while then walked over to some of the Spirit Sound kids.

"Who's in charge here?" The Commander inquired.

Jason pointed. "Ben Storm, he's over there."

Ben gave Pete a -- 'I thought you said we were good,' look and went to see what the officers needed.

"Let me do the talking, Pete instructed. "I'm sure they're just doing a look over."

Pete went over to see what was up.. "Hello officers, uh,"

"Ben Storm?" "Are you Ben Storm?"

"No, I am," stated Ben.

The elegant lady officer looked at Ben and at the scene around her. "How did you do this?"

"We have permits, Maam," Pete explained.

"No, I mean how did you get the community to come to this park?" "You've got rival gangs hanging out together and our man in the truck says that he has not seen a single drug deal go on while you all have been here. How did you do this?"

"I'm not sure. We're a church group from Colorado doing what we can to show these kids a bit of God's love," was all Ben could say.

"Pete here, set it up for us. He works with kids from the neighborhood."

The police commander looked over at Pete. "You could've put these kids in danger, you know?"

"The reason this is happening is because this wild man from Colorado believed something big could happen if he could convince the kids you see out there, to come to San Diego. Once they did, it's been God all along," Pete calmly explained.

She appeared to soften then gave Pete a stern look. "You got lucky."

The police entourage stayed and marveled at what was going on around them. Finally the Commander motioned to her officers. "Let's go. Unbelievable."

Ben had been sweating it out. "What was all that about?"

"Dude! Chill! I've got a good feeling about this. We got the attention of the City of San Diego and the Police in a good way."

Ben and Pete walked back to rejoin the kids. "Pete, I am not the wild man. You are. Next time, how about something a bit tamer."

"Yeah right, I know a wild man when I see one. We're twins. We don't do tame, Pete teased. Now let's wrap this baby up."

In the waning moments of the week of miracles and wonders the students took forever packing the bus. They stretched out every second so they could stay with the neighborhood kids longer. They had already stayed beyond the time they had planned and now with the sun casting long shadows across the park, there was no holding back the day. The time had come to leave. They had arrived at this park full of fear and apprehension, and were now leaving full of love and valor. Those at the park watched as the 1970 MC-7 drove down their street, rounded a corner and disappeared. They remained watching for several minutes as if somehow they could will the bus to shift into reverse and return. From somewhere in the crowd a child's voice prophesied; "They'll be back." Eventually, the group disbanded and went to their homes.

On the bluffs overlooking the Pacific that evening the staff and members of Spirit Sound were silhouetted against the setting sun. Some sat in groups, other chose to be alone. The reflecting and processing of thoughts continued way into the night . . . so late that Ben decided there would not be a curfew. He asked Ken and Tracy to hang back for safety reasons, and motioned for the rest of the staff to return to the dorms.

Walking to the dorms, Ben noticed that the moon was sitting low on the horizon and there was a warm breeze blowing. The talking had stopped so that the only sounds heard were of the waves against the rocks, the cries of seagulls, and the barking of the seals lying on the beach at the base of the cliffs. At that moment he would have given anything to be able to tap into each of the students minds and hear their thoughts. He wondered what he might hear. In time he would know that one thing the teens knew for sure was that they were going home so much different than they had arrived. It had been a communal experience. They had worked and performed together. They had traveled the same miles, eaten the same food, and stayed in the same places. Yet, the transformation that occurred was individual giving them their own story to tell. They would be reliable narrators giving first person accounts.

CHAPTER 47

With the bus packed, gassed up and ready to go, Ben stood at the front to share the daily devotional. He had reached in his Bible to get his notes when a small piece of paper fell out and floated to the floor. Cheri reached down to pick it up and handed it to him. The writing was faded and written in fine cursive. Ben instantly pictured the writer's face. It had been almost nine years since he had last seen her. He was so caught up in the moment that he forgot where he was and unaware of every-one waiting for him to begin his talk.

It was Annie's fake cough that brought him back to the present. Ben looked at the notes he had prepared for his talk and at the note written to him by Joyce. He thought about the stories the students had shared with him about the difficult situations they had endured growing up and as they navigated the angst of youth. Ben decided to pass on his prepared talk and focus on the message that Joyce had written to him as a teen and that had carried him during the difficulties of his life. He gave them some background so they would have context and then read a part of the note.

> "Ben, the God I know doesn't toy with us, and He will never waste our pain. Somehow, pain will always have a purpose, like some sort of preparation thing, maybe."

He called the student's attention to the reality of God's active participation in their lives even way before they had chosen to acknowledge Him. He talked about how they had been constant-ly in the process of preparation even when they were unaware. Although they had chosen to board the bus and hit the road, they had at the same time been chosen for the journey.

"Let me end by saying that pain is always tied to preparation and purpose. One of my favorite psalms puts it this way." 'You keep track of all my sorrows. You have collected all my tears in your bottle. You have collected each one in your book.'

The reminder that they had come into a relationship with One who launched the universe into existence, yet saw them . . . and knew them, hit home. Usually, after his talks the students were asked to take out journals and reflect. This time, Ben sat down and motioned for Earl to go. He placed the headphones of his Sony Walkman and thought about the truth in Joyce's words. She had not known it, but the words she had spoken had begun to break the bonds that had been holding him hostage. He wondered what adventures lay in store and what would be involved. When he got up to use the bathroom he saw that the teens were sitting with their favorite songs playing in their ears and with faces looking out of the windows or with eyes closed. The bus was filled with a stillness that lasted from the California coastline to the state line in the eastern desert.

When the silence broke, the question that had been ignored, but was resident in their minds was now the topic of discussion. Would they be able to maintain the change in their lives? Could they sustain it as they returned to their homes and schools? What about the parties they attended? Would they partake in the activities of the past? Where were the boundaries? They were working hard to come up with solutions to prevent them from slipping back into old patterns and habits . . . none that were viable came up. Ben went to the back of the bus where the students had gathered and listened in. The consensus was that they did not want to return to their homes and schools. They had concluded that given the pressures that they would face, it was inevitable that they would resort to what they knew and what would get them through the minefield of high school.

Then, Ramon's happened. The idea for a place where they could party and dance within a wholesome but cool venue sent them into a brain storming session. One idea led to another and in time a plan to transform their youth area at the church became reality. Ramon's started out in a small room then a wall was knocked out and the room was widened, and then it moved upstairs to the church's huge gallery. Ramon's would be a gathering place like the one the Apostle Matthew had set up for his friends. With a plan in place, Spirit Sound returned home a bit scared, yet ready to leave old habits behind and go on to live out what now burned within their hearts. The dances at Ramon's eventually drew in hundreds of teens.

CHAPTER 48

Two weeks after the group returned, Ben received a call. It was the call he knew he would get one day, but not on the day when he was still reveling in the after glow of an amazing trip.

The quiet man was dead. Ben's father had taken a fall and broken his leg. While he was in the hospital he developed pneumonia and passed away. His siblings asked him to attend the funeral and officiate a portion of it. He was pacing in his office when Annie walked in.

"What's wrong?" she asked.

Ben was amazed at how easily the words came out. "Sandi just called, my dad died."

He thought back to the last time he had seen the quiet man alive. He had wanted to be free of him, for him to just go . . . which he did. He had remained conflicted about the quiet man. Despite the many emotional wounds from the time he had lived with him, it was still difficult for him to acknowledge the anger. Gradually the feelings of hurt had changed to pity. The longing for a father and the opportunity to develop a relationship with his dad remained. Now it was final. He would never have a dad.

Annie remained at the door of the office. "Do you want to be alone?"

Ben did. He wanted to isolate, but he knew that was the old Ben's style. "Let's go for a run," he suggested.

They started out slowly jogging. When they arrived at the park, Ben left the concrete path and tore out across a field. Annie attempted to catch him, but he was running at a pace he had never run before. After a mile she caught up with him. Ben lay on the grass panting drenched in sweat breathing heavily. Annie lay down beside him. The sky had been overcast when they had left the apartment. Now thick black clouds packed the sky. With the threat of rain people began leaving the park until it was only Annie and Ben.

"You don't have to go," Annie offered. "The priest can do the service."

It was a great idea. Why subject myself to that, Ben thought. Maybe he could call Sandi and John and tell them he couldn't get away. It would be an easy thing to do. He knew going and seeing his relatives and his dad would open up all kinds of pain. They had been dead to him. What was it that Jesus said about, letting the dead bury the dead?

"Annie, why don't you go home?" "I'll be there soon."

She had only been gone thirty minutes when the clouds let loose their water. Lightning flashed and thunder lit the park up. Still Ben remained. His cries of supplication were lost in the deafening roar of the storm.

He rose and walked back home. The smell of fresh baked bread greeted him as he open the door. There was soup simmering on the stove. Annie sat in her favorite chair reading. She put her book down and went into the bathroom to get a towel to dry Ben off, then led him to the table and served him.

"I'm going to go. I'll wait until the priest does his part and I will close the service."

"Do you want me to go with you?"

"No, Annie, I'll be fine. I want you to meet Sandi and John under better circumstances."

Two days later Ben boarded a plane and descended into the land of his childhood. He had some time so he rented a car and went off to find St. Margaret's Home for Children from memory. All he remembered was the address and that it was off North Loop Road.

He took an off ramp and there it was. Ben had remembered the route they would take as kids when they went off on bike rides. He parked the car and walked from building to building. He walked through the fields and was saddened to see that the old cottonwood trees had been cut down and that the irrigation canals had been filled in with dirt. The Home was now empty of children. It had been transformed into an educational facility for Catholic Parishioners. Ben thought of Rodrigo and the first day he had become a resident of the Home. Instantly, he was catapulted into the past as scenes of the seasons he had spent at this place played in his mind.

The Home had been a place where summers were spent running barefoot chasing dragonflies through irrigated fields of alfalfa, while watermelon juice streamed down their faces. Summer meant that the Fourth of July was near. It was barbeque season with burgers and hot dogs, all washed down with drinks made from fizzies and served out of an ice-cold metal tumbler. It was a time of war and the battling with one of their nemesis, Miguel, the maintenance man who more than once thwarted the best conceived plans of Ben and his friends.

Fall was the season of wasp wars with its resulting swollen eyes, lips, and other wounds from the scrimmages in battling the hornets, and wasps. It was football and listening breathlessly to Notre Dame playing Michigan on the hand held AM battery powered radio. Afterwards Ben and Rodrigo would head out to the fields to emulate the actions of the players broadcasted by the radio announcers. The challenge was to squeeze out all that was left of Indian Summer, by staying outside as long as possible and trying to ignore the obvious and ominous arrival of the first day of school. Eventually, the only available option was to accept the inevitable and hang on to the hope of the big feast --Thanksgiving, and the four days of reprieve from the classroom.

In winter, the wind blew bitter and it chaffed the faces and hands of the kids and severely cutting into their time outdoors. The thrifty Nuns used Petroleum Jelly to rub in to the hands and cheeks of everyone until they felt liked greased pigs at the county fair. The secret in winter was to run anytime they had to go from one cottage to the other, or to the dining hall so their ears wouldn't fall off. Ben hated how the world was reduced to the colors, gray, brown or white and varying shades of each. His sole solace was that winter brought the season of wonder and the mystery and celebration of Christmas with its midnight masses and mountains of gifts donated by local merchants and benefactors from all walks of life.

Spring arrived blustery and bursting forth with the flowers of the season and the greening of the lawns and fields that had lain dormant all winter. Spring meant Easter and that everyone would be carted around to various charity events sponsored by college sororities, The Lion Club, even the nearby military base of Fort Bliss put on an egg hunt for the children of the Home. It was easier to accept this kindness when they were younger. But as they grew into teens, they began to feel self-conscious and more than ever like a charity case so that in time, Ben and the older kids began to dread these events along with arrival of mounds of leftover pack-ages of Peeps donated by any store that was unable to unload those sickening globs of yellow goo.

Spring was also the beginning of baseball season. Ben and his friends would carefully taken out their baseball gloves, which had hibernated under their bed mattresses all winter. In the fall, they had oiled and placed a baseball in the pocket and then tied them snug with string and laid them to rest for the winter. It was almost a religious ceremony and a ritual that Ben performed every spring as he and the other boys carefully unwound the strings and removed the ball – with the results being that the pockets of the gloves were now well formed and ready for the season. The final step of the ritual was to take these sacred icons with them on out-ings to watch the local Semi-pro team, hoping for a stray ball to come their way.

A Mocking bird's loud scolding brought Ben back to the present. He came upon the cinder block container that had been used to burn the trash generated by the Home. He laughed out loud when the memory of the time the boys had hid left over fireworks from the previous 4th of July. The boys concealed themselves in the ditch across from the incinerator and waited for Miguel, the maintenance man to arrive. It had been their most epic prank. The poor man had been casually tending to the fire when the blasting began. He immediately fell to the floor. Later that day Ben and his friends realized that they could have given him a heart attack. In the end, they were discovered and spent hours picking weeds under the boiling west Texas sun.

Ben left the Home and drove to Our Lady of the Valley Parochial School where he had spent seven wonderful years. When he could no longer delay the reason for his trip, he returned to the car, looked up the address of the funeral home and drove off.

The chanting of the Rosary that was being said in honor of the quiet man echoed into the hallway as Ben arrived. The people gathered, responded in a refrain as the priest led them in the Hail Mary. Relatives that Ben had not seen for years sat solemnly and wept softly. He saw Sandy and John sitting in the front pew and went to join them. After the priest finished, he stood and prayed a last prayer over the quiet man, then came over to where the quiet man's children sat, and offered his condolences.

When the priest left, Ben walked to the podium. He stood looking at the crowd unable to speak. It wasn't that he was choked up, or consumed with sadness. He didn't know how to start. Eventually he settled in and began by thanking the relatives and friends for coming. He began to eulogize a man he had not known with the few facts he had discovered about him. He began by honoring the quiet man for his military service, and as the man who along with his wife had given him and his siblings the gift of life. He spoke of his relationship with the quiet man's brothers and sister. Ben also spoke about the quiet man's broken heart from the loss of a love from which he had never recovered. When he was finished he went over to stand at the head of the casket and invited the guests to pay final respects. Where people had been previously weeping quietly, their cries were now audible. Ben had personalized the service and spoken of a man they had known and loved. His words had touched their hearts and released their grief.

As the people were returning to their seats, Ben turned to face the casket. He looked down at the quiet man remembering the countless opportunities he had given the man to be a dad. As a junior in college while in therapy Ben encountered a devastating truth. He had casually mentioned to his therapist that his dad was in town and had been encouraged to go visit him. The visit was exactly what Ben had anticipated. He returned to therapy and shared the experience and the response of the quiet man. After a long silence he heard . . . "you're never going to be a son to that man." The words hit him hard enough to knock the air from his lungs. Suddenly tears flowed and fell on his lap. He cried long and powerfully. When he was able to gather himself, the therapist quietly assured Ben that though the quiet man would never fulfill his role, Ben would in time experience being a son in several vicarious ways. He reminded Ben that he had a Father in the relationship he had with God. He predicted that one day Ben would marry and perhaps her father would become his father, and finally, if he were to father children, he would be the father to them that the quiet man had never been to him. In that moment he could only hope, but in time he would discover that all that the therapist had predicted would come to be. Ben placed his hand on the quiet man's and said softly: "We all missed out on so much."

The service closed with Ben leading the guests in a prayer committing the quiet man's mortal remains to the earth and his soul into the loving arms of God. After the service he spent some time talking with his family and then left to catch his plane. It was only when he was inside the rental car that he bowed his head and wept.

CHAPTER 49

Annie was waiting by the curb when Ben walked out from the airport lobby. He loved so much about her. He loved her smile . . . that and her green eyes. She had a way that settled him and reassured him when his world had gone bonkers. He gratefully slid in next to her.

"I am so glad to see you. Have you eaten?"

They were busy admiring each other when a traffic cop tapped on the window. Annie put the car in gear and peeled away from the curb. "Where to?"

"Round the Corner?"

The burgers arrived and remained on the plate. Ben related his trip to the Home, his school and the quiet man's service. He was glad that he had gone. Although he had returned with some residual feelings and a lack of closure, something had changed in him . . . and it was for the good.

Ben reached for his malt, stuck two straws into thick cream and leaned over towards Annie. "Shall we sip?"

Annie had been unsure of how the trip might affect Ben. She could see now that he had made the right choice. She relaxed and started munching on onion rings. In between bites Annie filled Ben in on what had been going on.

"Pete called. He wants you to call him pronto!"

"Did he tell you what's it's about?"

"No, he just said he needed to talk with you."

At the first hint of daylight, the birds in the yard went off. They were the most reliable alarm. It had been the same when Ben was living in the orange orchard. He reached over for Annie, but she was already up. Ben had just grabbed her pillow and covered his head in an attempt to drown out the bird's noises, when Annie came into the bedroom.

"Ben?" "Sorry, but it's Pete."

"Pete!"

"Bro, remember that female police Commander we met the last day we were at the park?"

Ben sat up in bed. "Pete, is this good news or are we in trouble?"

"It's all good. We started something big." Pete announced loudly.

"What?"

"Check it out. Two weeks after you guys left San Diego, the City came in and put a portable pool in the park for the kids. That's not all -- they also started a lunch program in the gym. I think that female police Commander that talked to us, got it going."

Ben jumped out of bed, "That's fantastic!"

"There's more. Remember Gail at Amor? She decided to add the park to the list of ministry projects her organization supports. The park is packed with kids every day and there's so much going on there that the gangs moved on. Bro, God used us to give the park back to the community!"

"Tell me you're not messing with me, Pete. You're serious?"

"Seriously. I have a feeling we haven't seen anything yet."

Ben hung up the phone and walked over to the window. He drew open the shades, opened the window and let out a huge shout. He found Annie and told her the amazing news.

Nineteen Years Later . . .

CHAPTER 50

Ben and Annie were staying at a hotel while attending a conference in San Diego. They were close to the neighborhood where they had spent five summers with Spirit Sound. Ben decided to find Pete. After a long search He found the church Pete was working at and dialed the number.

"Pete Contreras, please."

A familiar voice came on the line. "Ben, where are you?"

"Here in San Diego -- Annie and I are at a conference and staying close to where we did the park gigs. Do you have some time to get together and go to the park?"

"No problem. I'll come get you guys."

On the way to the park Pete and Ben chatted about all that had gone on in their lives since they had last seen each other. They almost missed the off ramp.

"Bro, get ready for this."

The car rounded the corner and stopped in front of an elementary school. Ben looked out of the window. When Pete parked, Annie and he got out. Nothing looked familiar. Ben looked down the block.

"Where are we?"

"We're in the hood, bro."

"Where's the park?"

"You're looking at it. They built this school on it. It's called, Rosa Parks Elementary. Get in the car and be prepared to be amazed."

Pete drove Ben and Annie to the back of the school where a huge park and sports complex had been developed.

"I think that once the city and some big dog business guys saw that the churches were investing in the area, they got behind it. It helped that you guys kept coming back. See over there? That's the San Diego Community College Extension building, and next to it is the Police sub station. You and your bunch came and got in the middle of it all, and nineteen years later, BAM!"

Ben and Annie stood with wonder on their faces. It was beyond good news. It was magnificent news. Pete had come into their lives and been the right guy at the right time. Long ago a seed had been planted to prepare Ben for this and many more adventures. Nothing that had happened to him in his youth had been wasted. The same was true for all who had participated in the initial trip. It had been God's pleasure to include them all in His grand journey. They just had to say they'd go and be willing to be put in the middle of it all . . . "In the midst of the village."

Outside of their hotel room stood a mighty Mulberry tree. Its abundant branches served as a covering over them. On the last night of the conference, Ben inched up close to Annie as they sat on the balcony listening to the wind rustling its leaves. Safe and snug under its canopy of green, the great tree lulled the two to sleep.

The End.

Epilogue

I n June of 1990, thirty-four adventurers, their rookie youth pastor, his great staff, and a retired principal, agreed to hop on a bus and head west. In the process they bumped into a modern John the Baptist, Pete Contreras, an urban youth pastor in San Diego. They had no idea the part they would play in setting in motion the transformation of many lives and an inner city neighborhood in a San Diego suburb. Before High School Musical, before Glee, before Pitch Perfect, there was -- Spirit Sound.

Pete Contreras continues to do amazing transformative urban ministry working with the youth and families of San Diego and beyond. He is a national speaker and developer of urban ministry pastors and staff. The park at City Heights where Spirit Sound began their work is now an ongoing outreach to the community serviced by his church and youth groups from around the United States.

Ben and Annie are in reality, Brian and Pamela Sky. The author felt self-conscious writing about himself and took the name Ben simply because every Ben he had ever know happened to be a nice guy. After working in healthcare, mental health, marketing, and ministry Brian followed Pamela into education. Today they serve in their schools in Colorado. While serving as a McKinney-Vento representative working with homeless students in the school district, Brian set up a nonprofit organization that reaches out and equips homeless teens in the schools in Colorado, while speaking nationally about the situation concerning homeless students. Currently Brian teaches high school students who are mostly migrants, immigrants or refugees from Northern and Eastern Africa, Central America, Mexico, The Ukraine, The Philippines, and other students from the plains of Eastern Colorado.

Research shows that as high as ninety-two per cent of the homeless teens living on the streets are there not because they are rebellious, suffering from conduct disorders, or mentally ill. Teens make the difficult decision to take to the streets as an attempt at self-preservation. Such was the case with Brian. Once he realized that if he were going to make it in the world, it would have to be up to him, he gathered his thirty-six dollars, his sleeping bag, a small suitcase, and moved into the orchard.

The longer a teen is homeless, the more likely they are to experience a host of negative consequences. Homeless youth living on the streets suffer from high rates of depression and post-traumatic stress disorder. They are more likely to fall victim to sexual exploitation when compared to young people who are not living on the streets, more likely to contract HIV and/or STDs due to increased likelihood of sexual exploitation, rape and sexual assault. In addition, they have higher rates of a variety of mental health symptoms including anxiety, developmental delays and depression resulting in elevated risk for suicide attempts. In the affluent city where Pamela and Brian live, there are over a thousand homeless teens scattered throughout the schools. This fact is most likely true of cities all across America.

Unlike many of the teens on the street Brian survived his homelessness with minimal negative effects because he was able to bring friends, and significant adults alongside him and lean on the foundation that his faith provided. He was one of the fortunate ones.

Acknowledgements

T
hank you to all the amazing people beginning with my wife Pamela (Annie) who gave me the gift of encouragement and her ever-constant love. My sons Evan and Nathan, the wild boys who make my life such a sweet adventure. To Lilly, my friend and sister since eighth grade and to her parents, Harold and Velma Sommers who took me in and gave me a place to lay my head. Joyce Volman for all the hope and healing you helped usher into my life. To Dave Fussell, Donald Lesika, and Ernie Marjorum who gave me shelter yet never told a soul. To Jay Rosson and Debbie Furnish for the extensive editing, Barry Netzley, Pamela Sky, Leah Goergens, Judy Castro, Becky Cleveland, Lilly Craig, and Betsy Elliot for the hours spent reading, and offering advice as I wrote. The 1990 Spirit Sound crew ---- you were the inspira-tion for this book. To Earl Knox who drove us thousands of miles, and to Earline for sharing him with us all those years. To my friend Pete Contreres, who without him so much of the story would be incomplete, to Ken, Dennis, Gary, and Tom as well as all my high school friends who were part of the journey during those years. To Father Stephens and The Sisters of Charity of the Incarnate Word,

for speaking words of life to me which provided a foundation for me when the storms blew later on in my life. To Mr. Lee Southard who without his generous gift, this trip may have never happened. Thanks to all the member of the '91- '95 Spirit Sound members and the youth groups from '87-'96. To Lee Graziano, who gave me my first job, and set me free from the bonds of poverty. To Owl, who shared her majestic tree, and to my Lord Jesus Christ, who loved me and gave his life for me.

In addition to teaching and writing, Brian speaks around the country during the summer advocating for the thousands of homeless students in schools across the United States. You can call him direct at 970-227-1980 or email him at brianjsky@gmail.com to schedule a talk, or to share your thoughts and experiences con-cerning this book or homeless students.

CPSIA information can be obtained
at www.ICGtesting.com
Printed in the USA
FSHW011443150119
55020FS

9 780692 959046